# the Lord looking down in pity

a novel by gene engelman

Copyright © 2016 Gene Engelman
A work of fiction, All rights reserved

ISBN: 0-9964578-2-8
ISBN-13: 978-0-9964578-2-8

Special Thanks to my friends
Annie and Alex,
John and Joy,
And especially Merrie.

This book is a work of fiction. Any references to historical events, real people, or locales are used fictitiously. Other names, characters, locales, and incidents are the product of the author's imagination, and any resemblance to actual incidents or places or persons, living or dead, is entirely coincidental.

All rights reserved, including the right to reproduce this book or portions thereof in any form whatsoever. Please share the ideas, but do not share the book.  Thanks.

Cover photos by author.

# contents

# i meet a fallen angel

He must have been handsome once. He had an old tan, and around his eyes he carried the deep lines of one who has faced the sun. He had a broad forehead, high cheekbones, a puggish nose. Evidently he came from good stock. Thin lips and the hint of a smile complemented a strong chin. All in all, he had a nice, harmonious face.

The trickle of blood issuing from the corner of his mouth simply added character. And his hair—pure white—the fall had mussed it, half combed-down-neat and half sticking-up-crazy, gave him an aura of excitement, as if there were ideas in that head of his, half-crazy, half-profound, that would unlock mysteries. He looked so peaceful stretched out on the gravel by the side of road—I thought him a fallen angel.

But that was then, a long time ago. I was young, and I had read Kerouac. And I had believed him, and this road was my romance.

Beatific? No. Beat and broken was closer to the truth. He'd peed himself in the truck. He stunk of piss and sweat and booze. He wore a dirty, blue blazer. One of the sleeves was coming off at the shoulder. Not enough coat for the road. I knew what it was like. On the road, after a few days without enough sleep and food, you get cold. Cold even with the sun shining down. I was learning.

He was breathing. He wasn't dead. The fall didn't kill him. The driver had tossed him from the shotgun side of a cab-over. It must have been a good six feet. "Here catch," the driver yelled after ejecting me without ceremony. I tried to protest. I didn't have anything to do with him. Didn't even know he was in the sleeper till he'd pissed himself. I had assumed that the stench in the cab was the driver. Or maybe me, I'd been a few days without a shower.

"Catch," and the trucker kicked my pack out the door. The old man followed. I didn't catch. I dodged. Glad to have my stuff. Amazed at my new companion.

The truck pulled off. Two shifts up the road the door opened. I ran up. The driver had reconsidered. I didn't want to get stuck out here. He was a good guy. I was relieved. I hadn't seen another car for quite a while. No farms, no stores, gas stations, nothing. Barely even pavement on the old road. It was getting dark. I huffed up, and the driver leaned out. "Catch." The old man's pack flew out. The door closed, and the big cab bounced away. Shift. Shift. Shift. Shift. And gone.

I didn't know what the hell to do. I should have just shouldered my pack and walked away. Left the sonofabitch lying there. But I didn't, couldn't. I was young and full of the romance of the road.

The drunk had a ragged rucksack with an old-style, quilted sleeping bag strapped on. I saw his canteen and figured, that's what you did to revive someone, splash some water on their face. So I did.

He woke up fast.

"JesusMaryJoseph. What the hell? What the hell ya doing? Wasting good booze. Gimme that. What ya doing with my stuff?"

He was standing in a flash—ready to do battle, prepared to meet whatever challenge life threw at him. Wiping his face, licking his hand. "Gimme that!" His eyes were beautiful, wild, feral. He fixed on me, breathing hard.

Then his body relaxed, eyes softened. He looked at me and smiled. I suppose he saw that I was benign. Or maybe just weak.

He looked me up and down, took a swig from his canteen, looked up and down the road. "Got a smoke?" I did and gave him one and lit one myself. He lit his match by folding the cover over and pulling the match out and flicking it to fire with one hand, then brought the flame up to trembling lips—the dancing cigarette steadied with his other hand braced against his chin. It was a neat trick. A trick I would practice, and later adopt, right down to the trembling lips.

He took another swig.

"Where the hell are we?" he asked.

"In the woods," I answered.

He looked me up and down again. "Stupid?" he asked.

I didn't reply.

"Stupid. Ya think I'm stupid?"

"Trees. Trees! I can see the damn wood!" He reached into the inside pocket of his jacket, pulled out a comb and ran it through his hair from front to back as a sort of pause to consider his situation. Then, "What the hell? Where we headed?"

I hesitated. He didn't wait for my reply.

"Don't matter. Where don't matter. Shanghaied is as Shanghaied does. When's the only thing. When we goin' get going?"

He brushed himself off. He picked up his pack and looked at it, then at me. "Must be some place just up the road. Where'd you say?"

"I don't know." I really didn't know where we were, not exactly. "The driver said something about a shortcut. He said that he used to haul cranberries. Then we got here out in the gravel. The road kinda fell apart. The pavement ... I wasn't paying attention."

"Cranberries? Cranberries? The hell."

"That's what he said, 'Cranberries.'"

The old man shook his head.

"Which way we going?"

I pointed east. The old man looked up the road, then turned and looked west toward a majestic line of thunderheads. A spring storm was headed our way.

"Didn't see nothing back there?"

"Just trees."

"Whew ... trees ... trees again.

"Hey. You ain't no Frenchie. I was in some cafe. Cafe nice an' cozy. Man had a bottle. Can-a-dee. Montréal. Where the hell?"

"No, we're not in Montréal." We were a long way from Montréal, so far I couldn't imagine him asking about it. "We're not even in Canada," I added. "We're in Jersey, South Jersey, Pine Barrens."

"I'll be damned and delivered. Don't look like no Jersey to me. How the hell? No matter. See any cars out here?"

"No, nothing."

"Hell of a thing, stuck out here in nowhere with some stupid kid. Whew. I need a nip.

"Hoist the hook an' cast her off.

"Cast her off to Hell."

He took a swig, then tucked his canteen in his rucksack and hoisted it on his shoulder and started walking east. Broken pavement and dusty gravel stretched through walls of low pines, straight and empty. I fell in beside him.

"What ya doing there?

"Don't know nothing, do ya? Get over there on the other side."

I didn't move. I didn't know. Maybe I smelled bad? Maybe, who knows?  He saw me hesitate.

"You know Mutt and Jeff?"

I didn't. And he saw I didn't.

"Burns and Allen? You know 'em?

"Abbot and Costello?

"Adam and Eve?"

I didn't see the point.

"Team, boy. They's a team. We's a team. You gotta look. Share and share alike."

He went on to tell me to walk down the other side of the road and to look for stuff on the ground that people had lost or thrown out of cars. "Found a diamond ring once," he explained. "Set me up for two weeks. Bunked in a real nice hotel right next to the old Trocadero. Two weeks. Whiskey. Wine. Women. Good times. Good booze.

"Gotta be a story in that ring. Eh?

"You see a car, you stick out your thumb."

"What if it's going the wrong way?"

"No wrong way. No wrong way out here. Squall ah coming. Which way don't matter."

I supposed that he was right. Who knew where this road led? Or which direction was mine? I walked on, looking for whatever I might find.  After all, that was the whole point, right? To find Jack and Neal's *It* somewhere on my road. Who knew what road it would be?

"Found a fifty dollar bill once," he said. "Fifty dollar bill in the grass.

"Imagine some good ol' boy was lookin' at his fifty dollar bill, and 'Oops' out the window she goes.

"Didn't even look back.

"Maybe he did. Maybe he circled around and looked but he just couldn't find it. Good for me. Eh?

"Found a gold tooth. Gold tooth shining in the sun. Sitting in a gutter. Got some money for that one. Gold, set me up for two weeks. Hotel on Vine. Block from the Troc. That's burlesque boy. Gurly-girls. Two weeks on that gold tooth.

"Gotta be a story in that tooth."

I didn't respond. My new partner didn't enjoy silence.

"Found me a whole set of dentures. Dentures laying in the road. Gold tooth too! Man driving down the road and 'Oops,' opens his mouth and out they go. Think he'd go back. Get em. Eh?"

He was like a feral, third-world dog doing all its tricks to get your attention so you'd give it the heel of your sandwich. I had no patience. I was young and not a little perturbed at the situation. This wasn't working out like the book. I said, "Maybe someone smacked him and knocked those teeth out of his head? Eh?"

"Knocked 'em out? Knocked 'em out?" He stopped walking and looked at me hard. "Why you got to be so mean? Just making conversation. Passing the time."

"You're scaring off the cars," I said.

We walked, and we walked, and there was nothing but road and trees and the thunderheads at our backs.

"WooWee. Lookiee here."

He'd found something.

"What?"

He laughed. "Dog shit. Pile of dog shit. Watch yo' step. Dog shit."

"How do you know it's from a dog?" I asked.

"I know my shit," he said and thought himself so funny that he said it again. "I know my shit boy. I know my shit."

I should have known better. I should have jumped out of the truck when it turned off the main road. But it was a good ride. This driver didn't say much. He mostly listened to the radio and drove mile after mile. I liked that. Sometimes they wanted conversation. Some wanted you just to listen. Some of them were pretty angry about the war, angry about the hippies and the long hair. Some were hippies and wanted you to roll them a joint. Some had good stories. Some of them wanted to freak you out with their stories. One guy had me take the wheel and whipped it out. When I drew back—and let-go of the wheel—he put my hand back on the wheel and said, "I gotta pee. You either hold the wheel or something else."  I held the wheel while he peed into a gallon jug. He was an okay guy, bought me a burger later, and we laughed about it. This latest one was just a guy who wanted to go home, deadheading, sans trailer, bobtail. I guess that's why he risked the broken pavement of our lonely backroad. But I didn't know about the other passenger, didn't know he'd previously picked up my new teammate.

"There're no dogs out here."

He nudged it with his toe. "Looks fresh." He turned to me with great sincerity. He smiled and flashed his eyes. "Since this here is a brand new partnership. And since youse the junior partner. I'm gonna be generous and give you this first prize we got."

We kept walking. Looking. He couldn't *not* talk.

"Fresh dog shit. Must be a house or a farm or somethin' here. Maybe we can get a bite to eat? Maybe get a ride outta here?

"Maybe find a roadhouse?

"Maybe find a bar?"

"Maybe find a diamond," I said back sarcastically. "Eh?"

I could feel the storm at my back. Thunderheads building fast in the west. Typical spring weather pattern. We'd be getting wet before sunset. We hadn't seen any cars at all. Who drove out here?

"You got an umbrella?"

"What?"

"Umbrella. Gonna be getting some rain. Where's that farm them dogs come from? Hell, maybe we's going the wrong way? Maybe we should turn 'round? Find that farm and them dogs."

I had an anorak in my pack. Not much good in anything more than a mist. A downpour two days before soaked me. Freezing rain had saturated it before I'd gotten under an overpass. No overpasses here, nothing to pass over. The pine on both sides didn't look like much protection either. Maybe we'd get a ride? Easier to get rides in bad weather, but it would be hard to see us out here in the rain and dark. We could have used a streetlight or two. Too bad I had the old guy with me. It would be harder to get rides with two, harder still with a shabby, old stumblebum. Impossible when there weren't even any cars.

"Lookiee here."

I could see that there was a break in the trees. The ghost of a track ran off to the north, two snaking impressions in the ground where tires had lately rolled. It was overgrown with brush and saplings. I crossed over to take a look. The young pines had been bent down fairly recently. Their broken stems showed bright yellow. Their needles were still green. Somebody in a car or pickup had driven over it and knocked down the fresh growth. I walked a few feet in, but couldn't see anything. It was just a two-rut track, probably went to nothing.

The squall line stretched across the western horizon, tremendous, heroic thunderheads rising out of it, the highest already beginning to flatten in the upper atmosphere. Dead west, a tower climbed toward the sun—dense with malevolent intent to blot out the day. The sun's corona held on, seemed to explode over the edge of the cloud with rays crimson against an azure sky, defiant against the cruel, dark tower. And then the sun was gone. I looked down, and the old man was holding up a big, wooden arrow. He was shaking it and pointing down the overgrown track like a character in a cartoon. Was this all an insane dream in the back of some rolling ride? No, not a cartoon dream. The arrow was a wrecked sign he had found in the underbrush. A bit of white paint still clung to it. He shook it once more and tossed it down. It was growing dark, but the storm was still a while off. We had some time. I wanted to stay on the road. Maybe a ride? But the old man was already headed off up the old track. "What ya looking at?" he said impatiently. I was looking at the surreal sign. He stopped. "Them dogs. This here's where they live. That's a farm road. Farm up the road." He unshouldered his rucksack and opened it and took a swig from his canteen. "You coming boy?"

I wasn't so keen about walking in on some farmer —folks didn't settle here because they wanted to be sociable. I could have just kept on walking. I'd been cold and wet and alone before, but that was out on the highway with cars passing and lights in the distance. Here in the pines, not a soul around, it was desolate and lonely, and even a beat-up drunk seemed like some connection to the world. Besides, we were a team, right?

"Hey, hey, get a move on," he called. "Come on there, boy. We gotta find us some shelter at the farm." His fiction of the farm became his reality. A few steps and he turned back to see if I was following. "Ain't got all day. God damn it, boy." I could tell he was scared. I could see flashes in the clouds. Too far still for thunder. "Jesus, come on."

I didn't leave him.

The trees closed in on us. This little track was overtopped by branches. Two rows of tall, slender trees lined the route. It was like being in a long hallway, much darker than the gravel road. "Never go into dark woods," someone had warned me when I was a kid. That's what came to mind as I followed the flopping, old boozer.

"Hail clouds," he said. "Hell boy. It's hail. Hell hail. Get it?" He laughed at his joke, joyous to see me following. A warm breeze from the east kissed my cheek. The clouds were sucking in air. Too warm, too humid, I could feel the pressure-drop in my soul. The thunderheads had taken my sunlight, now they wanted my air—greedy bastards of sky and darkness.

"Hail! Hell! Seen a whole herd of longhorns in Dakota struck down dead. Hailstones big as balls. Big as balls. Balls big as baseballs. Raining down death on them poor critters. Seen it with my own eyes. Kill ya dead. Raining death on them poor sonsofbitches." There was desperation in his voice. He reached out to pull my arm and speed me, thought better of touching me and stopped. Looked at me pleading, "Come on boy, hurry."

He was a scared, old man who didn't want to be alone in the storm. What could I do? So I ran with him down the track. I didn't want to be alone either. His fear was infectious. It was getting very dark. Just a couple of days before I'd seen the aftermath of a tornado in Wisconsin—a surreal patch where the trees had been knocked over. A broad swath of destruction, fifty yards wide crossing the highway, disappearing into the woods in both directions—trees flattened like stalks of grass, big trees, old, second-growth. It was like a giant hand had gone thru and brushed the pines aside.

"Paul Bunyan," I had joked with the guy who had given me a ride.

I had just passed through Minocqua, Paul and his Blue Ox, Babe, were on my mind.

"*Finger of God*," said my ride, a local, dressed head-to-toe in white, driving an orange Pinto. "That's what the meteorologists call it, *The Finger of God*. It was an F5," he went on to explain. "Top of the friggin' scale." When he had seen me he had slammed on the brakes and slid onto the shoulder and skidded like hell soon as his wheels left the pavement. I sprinted up to him. Hesitated when I saw how he was dressed. I thought he was an inmate escaped from the asylum or an acolyte from the Krishna. It turned out that he was a baker headed home from work. He needed someone to roll one while he drove. "God's way of reminding you who's in charge," he said in reference to the swath of destruction. "Nothing you can do about it."

At the time I had thought the *Finger* was simply a reference to the destruction, the sweep of a great digit across the landscape that destroyed everything. Running from the storm with the old man I found another, more philosophical meaning—a little message from God perhaps? A *Finger* for the unbelievers? A demonstration of what He can do when He wants to?

The old drunk stopped. "What now?" Someone had emptied a pickup truck load of construction debris in the middle of the track—drywall, odd scraps of plywood, bits of 2x4, pink insulation—not demo, but what was left after a fresh build. Others had added to it with household trash, garbage bags spilling out coffee filters and milk cartons, stuffed animals and faded plastic children's toys. Off to the side I saw a couch and a toilet bowl. Party trash had been dumped too, beer cans, butts, bottle cases, pizza boxes, whatever. A couple of yards beyond was another, an older pile with plaster and lath and window frames and again, a discarded toilet. Small trees had been given time to grow through this ancient debris, quite a little dump, enough to stop any traffic. But not us. The old man scampered around the pile, driven by fear of the storm.

The hallway of tall trees ran on in the dark woods. This track on the far side of the dump was well overgrown, but we could follow where it had once been a road. Some fallen pines had to be scrambled over, down and dead a long time ago, their branches brittle and needles brown. I didn't want to lose the old man. We went on and on, the track twisting, the old man pausing for a moment to follow it and then go on. He kept peering ahead, jogging with an odd step to keep his pack from slipping off his shoulder. Then there was a lake and a cabin, barn, pilings, the skeleton of a pier. It had been something once. Antlers nailed over the door of the cabin said it was a hunting camp. And the lake? Good fishing? The place was old and overgrown, abandoned years, perhaps decades, before.

The old man had stopped, but he wasn't looking at the camp—he was looking at his shoe.

"Dog shit. Shit." I looked down. I'd just missed a pile. There was a lot, some dried-out old, some fresh. The old man was leaning on a tree. He had a stick and was scraping shit off his heel.

"There's nobody here. Nobody's been here for a long time. There're no dogs. Just some deer," I was saying, referencing the abundant excrement. "It's from some deer or raccoons or something."

"It's dog shit, boy. I know my shit. Know my shit," he was giddy, suddenly laughing, drunk with salvation. Happy now that we'd found shelter. We were saved. And I didn't know it then, but he knew he had an extra bottle stashed in his pack to get him through the night. That was what mattered to him. We'd found a place, a cabin where he could drink and sleep it off. That's all he wanted. Just a few more hours. "Maybe it's from some coyotes, or foxes, or a pack of wolves coming to eat ya," he said with a smile. "Maybe it's that Jersey Devil folks always talking about. Maybe we done found his secret camp." He threw down the shit-scraping stick and took a swig from his canteen. "Hell. What ya waiting for. Let's go inside an' introduce ourselves." He headed to the cabin.

"Watch your step," he added with an, "Eh?"

The cabin door was closed with a padlock and hasp. Clearly there was no one home to introduce ourselves to. My traveling companion gave a few knocks, then a couple of pounds with his fist, and then a few shoves. He put his weight into it a couple of times. Then, suddenly concerned, he violently threw himself into it. The door came off at the hinges, the lock and hasp holding. "Ain't nobody home."

The windows were covered with wooden shutters. In the dim I could just make out a table and chairs, an iron stove in the corner. To let in some light, I pulled open a window and released the clasp on its shutter and swung the wood outward. It didn't help much. The sky was dark. The old man struck a match and lit a big, white candle that was on the table. "Kinda cozy," he said. With the candlelight, I could see that it was as if the owner had just stepped out a minute ago. But my finger touched to the table's dusty top spoke of a long absence. Somebody had left and never had the chance to return. And people had forgotten about it.

On the back wall, above a counter with tin sink and cast iron pump, was a cabinet closed with a small padlock and hasp. The old man went right to it and gave it a tug. "Wonder what they got locked up?" he said knowingly. "Let's see here." He looked around and stopped his eyes on the poker for the stove. In a second he was prying off the hasp. "There we go. WooWee." He held out a half-bottle of whiskey. "Regular liquor store in here. Top shelf." I looked in. There were a half-dozen bottles with varying degrees of liquor. The old man took a swig from the one in his hand. "Gotta find us some glasses. Got another smoke, son?"

I gave him a cigarette and lit one for myself. A gust of wind blew through the doorway. The storm was really coming on. There was a lantern on the counter and next to it a can with screw-top spout, *Kerosene* painted on its side. Whoever had left this place couldn't have made things easier for us. I got the lantern going as another gust came in and extinguished the candle. "Just in time," the old man said. "Now 'bout them glasses?

"Regular summer camp," he said and sat at the table. I opened another cabinet, not locked this time. There were a couple of big jars with saltines and another with some kind of cereal, maybe oatmeal that had seen better days. There were some cans with crumbling paper labels, others drab green with words printed in black, but I was looking for glasses. Next cabinet held the plates, cups, bowls, glasses. I got two of the latter, and he poured us each a shot.

Noticeably colder, another gust shook the door and the shutters and the cabin and the trees. I looked outside. The first big drops were falling. It was dark. What the hell. I was trapped for now. I drank my whiskey down in a gulp. It was a Jack Kerouac moment. It was the adventure I had been seeking. The road. The whiskey. The storm. The cabin. I didn't consider how it had ended for Jack and Neal. This was a romance of youth—-*On The Road* not *Big Sur*. *Dharma Bums* not *Satori in Paris*. Fear of the storm gave way to relief. The whiskey burned as it went down. I choked and spit a little up. The old man looked at me sympathetically. "You need a little creek water in that, son. Why don't you get us a splash before the rain."

It wasn't a question. It was an order of sorts. The old man was taking charge now. He was loaded enough to have his confidence. Sitting at the table with his bottle of *Old Grand-Dad*, he was home.

There was an enameled pitcher ready on the counter. I put it under the pump and pumped hard. For my trouble I got nothing but creaks from the old iron. "Gotta prime it boy." I had no idea what he was talking about. "Gotta get some water from the lake. I'll show ya." He pointed to the door and the lake.

I took up the pitcher and stepped into that surreal darkness that precedes a strong storm. It wasn't night, but it was dark and damp with the smell of rotting spring. The air was dead, the big drops had stopped for the moment, all the world was still but for distant flashes in the west. I walked to the lakeshore and turned toward the cabin, faced the west. The tree tops were silhouetted in silver bursts too far to hear. Then as I stood with my back to the lake and watched, the distant thunder came low and long, its crack flattened by time and distance.

I remember that calm, then the wind in the pines like the roar of trucks on the interstate. That's what it reminded me of, the roar of the interstate, and I had to get the water. The wind came through the pines and ripped across the lake in random gusts. There was no direction. All at once, gusts like bombs exploded around me. Big, well-spaced drops of cold rain fell on me and splashed in the water and cratered the white sand, and I thought of the old man's story of the hail and the white-suited baker's *Finger of God*—whose aftermath I had seen with my own eyes. Maybe it was the whiskey's doing, entranced, I was taking it all in like a dream. I watched a gust in the distance blow up a line of whitecaps. Another gust flattened out the little cove by the cabin. There was a float pulled up on the shore, its 50-gallon drums rusted and collapsed. By the edge of the ruined pier I saw a dog watching me. So the old man was right about the shit. Here was the shaggy culprit—a dog, the ugly mutt that surprisingly saves the day—a fine companion for our adventure.

"Hey pooch," I called. "Hey little buddy," called as I moved toward it.

The dog stared at me for a heartbeat, then raised its hair and snarled. I'd never seen a dog so ferocious. Not more that 20 pounds, but with a growl and baring of teeth that set me back on my heels. The world flashed and cracked at the same moment—the storm was on us—like a scene in a movie where the lightning reveals the beast. Another flash, the dog was gone. And the rain was on me.

My hair and shirt were soaked in the sprint to the cabin door. I was dripping.

"Just asked ya for a drop. Not the whole damn pond."

He was totally unconcerned. "Let me see a touch of that spring water." He poured an inch of whiskey in his glass and topped it with a half-inch of water. I did the same and took a sip.

"Just like summer camp. Eh?

I stood and leaned on the wrecked doorframe and looked out. In the flashes I watched the trees. Slim trunks swayed to and fro while branches dipped and rushed in a frenzy. Safe now, I could watch it for hours, the ultimate power of the sky, of nature at her best and at her worst. I wanted to find the answer in it. If I could just look at it long enough, see it clearly without the filters of past storms and of future storms and of metaphors of storms and winds and rains and flashes of insight, if I could only see it purely, I knew there was something important in it that I could believe. I wanted so desperately to believe. I thought of Jack and his time on Desolation Peak. I peered into the darkness between the bright bursts. I felt the rain splashing, the wind on my cheek. What had he seen there?

But I didn't have the patience. I got bored and went back to the old drunk and the bottle. I drank more drinks. I didn't eat much. I had some granola in a bag. We shared in handfuls. "Tomorrow we'll catch a mess of fish," he promised. "Snare rabbits. I can skin 'em good. Just like taking off a glove." I believed him.

"We'll live like kings." I figured he knew what he was talking about. The road had worn me out. It had only been a couple of days, but I was beat. I was accustomed to regular meals and a good sleep in my own bed every night. And I wasn't used to drinking hard liquor. The whiskey was going to my head. I didn't want to think or talk anymore, just to stop. There was a second room, small, with four bunks on the walls, two and two with a space between. I told him goodnight and put my pack up and climbed to an upper one, slid into my sleeping bag and listened to the old man quietly telling himself his stories while the now-gentle rain tapped the roof.

I slept soundly.

Years later I was in a bar telling them about the old man, and the company I was keeping agreed that I was crazy, naïve, stupid, "Hell, that odd cuss could have stuck a knife in ya, and ya'd never know ya never woke up." But he didn't, or I wouldn't have been drinking in that bar, nor would I now be telling you this story of my salvation.

# paradise found

Sensations evoke private memories of the past. Walking now on the beach, now some forty years removed from the events of this story, the chill that hugs my shoulders is an open highway and a morning-cold sun. And no matter what time has past, whenever I feel that chill embrace me, I am back on that Canadian highway. And I'm a young man, and I've got my own road ahead of me and joy at the freedom of my dawn. And I sleep on the ground and get up fresh without an ache or groan.

And there is no tomorrow on my highway. I take time easily. I flow with the universe. Fears of the future, of love and career and security and satisfaction, even happiness, are subsumed in the immediacy of a new town, the crest of a next hill, the expectation around that curve. And my life is all the short, perfect moments strung together. Now, as I write, I struggle to reconstruct those moments and relive the adventures of my youth, and I try to remember the mix of fear and courage that drove me on and the naïveté that opened my heart to adventure.

The kid working at the gas station lets me wash-up in the restroom while he opens. Coffee's black in the heavy, white mug he hands me. We sit with coffee-steam rising in rosy-red dawn and mist on the big lake, and he tells me of *his* trip across the Rockies, legs dangling from boxcar's door, blue flowers on the sunny hillsides, still snow in the deep cuts. Two gear-heads in a jacked TransAm pick me up. Salvation with a Hurst on the floor, I was freezing my ass off. Me and my pack, we hardly fit in the back. Hell-bent we scream for some backwoods bar to shoot pool and drink till I'm drunk and slip away as the fight over the banking 8-ball breaks out. I sleep in the woods. Headed to his second job, my ride has a wife with headaches and a thirteen-month old kid. A drunken couple argue about laundry, whites and colors, for seventy-five miles and an eight-pack of *Point*. A warehouse manager talks daily to his female counterpart halfway 'cross the continent on the WATTS line. It's been two years of talking. He's asked her on a date. He's driving two days. She'll meet him at the truck stop just off the 2nd exit for Montréal. She'll be next to the phone booths. She'll wear a green coat. A salesman who knows the score laughs at him. "Maybe it's a joke?" My ride worries all the way from Sudbury. He drops me at the truck stop, and I see her in her green coat running already toward his green sedan. Takes hours to hitch the last few miles into downtown. Some guy in a tattered suit holds a book and screams something incomprehensible. Tears down his cheeks. The same words over and over. A car pulls up, and a man gets out. He says something in French and slaps the crying-man hard. Gets back in his car and drives away. An attractive woman, short blond hair, tennis whites, a racket beside her, pulls her car up. She's stopped for the light. She looks at me, leans over, locks the passenger side door. Even now, when I hear that distinctive click of the car-door lock, I can see her, and I still shrug, and I still smile. I suppose she speaks French.

I dreamt of her that night and woke refreshed. The old man was passed out on the lower bunk, blankets half-wrapped around him. He had one arm sticking out straight over the edge and into to aisle between the beds, his hand turned upward in supplication. Empty glasses, bottles on the table, more on the counter, evidenced that the old man had drunk it all—all but a sharp-edged bottle full of something very green. I noticed an orange jar of instant coffee on a lower shelf of a cabinet. Better than nothing. I put a teaspoon in a mug and went out to the lake for some water. It didn't really dissolve in the cold lake water, but I sipped it anyway and lit a smoke.

The air was clean, washed by the rain. The apocalyptical frenzy of the night had exhausted itself. The sun was just topping the pines, throwing streaks of shadow across the calm water. We were on a cove at one end of a lake that disappeared around a wooded point and stretched, it seemed, well out into the north. On shore was a big, barn-like building with two sets of oversized doors. A garage? Boathouse? Dancehall? One corner had caved in. Young pines had taken root and climbed out.

The hand upturned stuck in my mind. He'd want some coffee, real coffee, so did I. The place was pretty well stocked. There must me some. I tossed the instant and went back to the cabin. I poked around the upper cabinets, found a bottle of gin that the old man had missed, laid it down behind some cans, then grabbed a dull-green can that had *Coffee* printed in black. It had a key and tab. I unpeeled the tab and the band that held the can tight. It was old, but it was coffee, real coffee, and it smelled fine.

Everything on the ground was wet. I remembered hearing, or reading, or seeing on television, that the dead branches on the underside of pine trees were good kindling. I went into the woods and gathered enough branches to get a fire going. As I walked back, hunched under the low pines, I caught a quick motion out the corner of my eye. By the time I turned it was gone. I thought of the mutt from the night before. I just got a glimpse, too big for that little dog. Anyway, we were in the woods, bound to be some animals.

The pine crackled to life quickly. Things were going well. I was quite proud of my woodcraft. I'd make the old man some coffee, then we could head back to the road. I heated the water with an old-style, enameled kettle, conveniently found in the cabin, which I simply put in the fire. I dumped in a handful of the coffee, let it settle a spell, wrapped my bandana around my hand for a potholder, and then carefully poured myself a cup of the hot joe. I figured we'd get back on the road, maybe have to walk a while. Surely there'd be rides out there during the daylight. I was anxious not to let the day go by.

"Time to get up. Come on," I yelled, almost guilty at breaking the quiet. "I made some coffee." And poured a cup for the old man.

No reply. So I went back to the cabin with his coffee. I called to him again.

The old man grunted, pulled his hand under his quilted bag and rolled over.

"Come on. I made coffee."

"Yeah. Yeah. Minute."

It was obvious that he wasn't going anywhere soon. I went out and lit another smoke and drank his coffee. I still had the motion of the road on me. I was thinking to up and shoulder my rucksack and walk out and be gone. But something held me back. Curiosity? Conscience? Who knows? He was nothing to me. He smelled bad. He'd gotten me booted off a good ride. He was a liability, much harder to get a ride with him along, maybe impossible. But as I sat and looked around, I felt the stillness. I didn't have any place I had to be. I had some time. I decided to wait until he woke up.

It was a simple, watershed-crossing of a moment— the crest of a gentle hill overtopped without even realizing it or the turning of a tide on a broad, shallow beach. It was not a well-considered, conscious decision. Not a decision that's obviously going to change one's life, like going to this college or that, or asking for a woman's hand in marriage, or having a child, or taking a job in California or New York or some Godforsaken South Dakota city. No, this was so subtle that I didn't even feel it, then one day I remembered and reflected and understood that it was this exercise of free will—this decision barely felt— which would come to define what I was, and what I would be, and, most importantly, what I am now.

Motion and sound from the big building caught my attention. A glimpse of brown disappearing. Something little? Rat? Raccoon? Possum? The ferocious pooch from last night? A tentative nose appeared from a crack where one of the big doors stood ajar. A bold fellow stepped out into the sunlight.

It was a puppy. Then more puppies, little black and tan puppies, still with short snouts and oversized paws, came stumbling out. I smiled at my little Paradise in the Pines. I remember that's exactly what I thought. I liked the alliteration. In retrospect, I should have wondered what puppies would have been doing out in the middle of the woods, but I didn't. It was all so dreamlike. I went over to the pups, bending toward them calling, "Here puppy. Here puppy." As I closed on them and bent down and reached out my hand I heard a quick rustle in the barn. A jolt on the door and a fierce nose with fangs pushed through. Mom! Another two inches, I would have been missing two fingers. It was a lovely, peaceful, pastoral moment of snarl and spittle.

While mom was pushing her nose through the crack to kill me and save her puppies, and I was appreciating that I still had five fingers and was stupidly watching mom's snarling snout, dad, a doberman, came around the corner of the building. In the instant it took me to realize his presence, another dog, a German shepherd, came around followed by the scruffy terror from the past night and others I didn't have time to inventory. I think the puppies were as surprised as I was. They had never seen a person before and had no experience, hence no fear of humans. But the others clearly had had some history with my species. The doberman, a big, angry head with huge teeth, stopped. He was the leader, and the others followed suit. I knew enough not to run. I backed slowly toward the fire and carefully, so carefully, picked up a stick that was burning on one end.

The dogs stood their ground—didn't advance. I realized that my stick would be futile against the pack. Was I supposed to stare them down? Or look away? I couldn't remember. I certainly couldn't outrun them. I took a step back. The doberman took a step forward. I kept backing away, waiting for the dog to charge. I don't think he wanted to hurt me, just to keep me away from the puppies. The ground was uneven, and I stumbled just a bit. The doberman tensed up. I saw the look in his eyes that I'd seen in the old man's eyes--wild, feral, ready to take on the world. I moved toward the cabin, slowly, carefully, quickly as I dared. The doberman and his minions watched, but did not charge. They held no malice, just wanted to protect their own.

I backed in the door and wrestled it shut as best I could. The old man stirred in the next room, leaning his elbow on the bunk.

"Wha'. What?"

"There're wild dogs out there. We need to leave. Get out!" I said not unexcitedly.

"What? Huh?" He rummaged around and pulled out a bottle with about two inches of whiskey in it, focused on it for two seconds, then, "Let a man sleep." I started to explain the dog situation to him. He put his hand up, palm out, to stop me, took a swallow of the booze, pushed himself up, tottered, leaned heavily on the upper bunk and looked around, found what he was looking for and made a lunge into the main room and toward the sink. He vomited hard into it, puking out the whiskey he'd just swallowed. He dry heaved a few times. His whole body shook, and a trickle of blood came from the corner of his mouth. He steadied himself with both hands hard on the counter. The veins and sinews stood out on his arms. He wiped the blood off his chin with the back of a hand and looked at it. "Gimme that bottle, boy." I gave him the bottle from the bed, and he took a slow, delicate swallow. He paused for a moment, holding it down. Then took in a little more. He was very careful this time.

"Okay," he finally said. "That's the girl. Slow and easy. Easy and slow." He looked down at the whiskey vomit in the basin as if it were a lost friend.

He smiled at me and took another little sip. "Dogs you say? Wild dogs? Long's they don't drink my whiskey, don't give a shit.

"Whew, some bilge we got ourselves in. Here now, who are you? What ya doing here?"

"What?"

"What?" The old drunk raised his voice a bit, mocking me. "What? What? You stupid? I asked you a question." All this while he looked around the room.

I didn't understand. Was he crazy? His greasy hair was twisted up and standing on end. Wearing a dirty tee-shirt with a hole under one armpit, pee-stained khakis, way too big and cinched with an oversized leather belt, he certainly looked crazy.

Then he caught himself. He was quite calm, if not a bit impatient with me. "Now, boy, exactly what's been doing here?" he inquired calmly.

"We're in a cabin. In the woods. There's a pack wild dogs outside. They're gonna eat us."

"Whew." He paused a moment to take it all in.

"Okay now. Now don't go messing with an old man. Cabin in the woods? And wild dogs gonna eat us? And we got us Bigfoot coming for breakfast?" he said with a smile.

"Jesus," I said. "There're wild dogs."

"Don't be taking the Lord's name in vain like that," said slowly. Whiskey was taking hold. "Lets us start from the beginning. You and I are here in this room. Room looks a little shabby. Got a sink and table. This your place, boy?" He looked around again. The window caught his eye. He took a peek. Without a further word he went over to the door and gave it a tug. It came crashing down, spinning on the hasp as he jumped aside and looked out and, "JesusMaryJoesph. Where the hell am I?"

"I told you, in the woods, in a cabin, in the Pine Barrens, dead end, South Jersey. The driver kicked us out. You pissed yourself. We came here in the rain. There's a pack of wild dogs. Don't you remember?"

While the old man was taking it all in, the doberman led three curs across the clearing in front of the firepit.

"JesusJoseph. And a good God damn. Shanghaied again." He stepped back into the cabin and peered out and then, with the pooches gone, stumbled into the sunlight, shaded his eyes with a hand. "Damned and delivered. I'll be dammed and delivered. How the hell I get here?"

"We came last night, remember?" I said. Before following him I stuck my head out looking for the dogs, who seemed to have disappeared.

"No. Last thing I remember I was at a bar. Bar down by some river or lake or ocean or some damn thing. Nice lady buying drinks. Chatting me up. In the city. I was in a God damn city down by the river.

People talking French. Montréal, that's where I was. Where in the hell?"

The old drunk walked out into the brightness, out toward the firepit and the circle of logs. He looked them over carefully, focused on the ground and the soil and weeds and fallen sticks and the young pines that were reclaiming the clearing. There was a fresh pile of dog shit behind one of the log benches. "Boy," he said, "You do your business over in the woods."

"It's the dogs!"

"Ain't sanitary. Gotta keep up appearances. Appearances 'round here, dogs you say?"

"In there." I pointed. "They were in there, over there." I pointed to the building with the big doors and collapsed corner.

"Dogs," he repeated slowly, lifting his gaze toward the trees and building and then noticeably shifting his eyes back to the sandy soil as if he didn't want to take it all in, as if not seeing would keep it all a dream, and if he didn't know he wouldn't be where he was. Or maybe he was just being scrupulous about not stepping in the dog shit, he hadn't put on shoes. His feet were bare.

"Wild dogs," he repeated and started walking over toward the big doors. Then before he reached them, his attention was drawn by the lake, and he turned toward it. "A lake, lake is nice." And it was nice, with just a hint of air drawing cat's-paws across the cove. "I was in bar, chatting up a nice lady. I need a drink."

He still had the bottle in his hand. He went slowly to the shoreline and sat down on a log and took a pull. "Got a smoke?" I gave him one. He pulled a book of matches out of his pocket and got the cigarette lit after a couple of tries. He looked at the matchbook carefully. He held it at arm's length and squinted. "Sometimes matches gives you a hint," he said cryptically. "Ain't nothing. I was chatting up some lady. Pretty lady, classy." He took another pull on the bottle and looked at what was left, the sun shining through it. "Talking French."

He finished the whiskey with a gulp, took a drag on the smoke, then tilted the bottle to his lips and let the last drops slide down into his mouth. "Thar she blows." He flung the bottle into the lake. "Bombs away." It splashed.  The sun caught the spray and a ring of ripples expanded and died. The bottle floated on its side for a time, then turned neck up. He watched and sighed and stood and shook himself, flicked the cigarette butt into the lake to join the bottle.

He suddenly stiffened, then snapped around toward me.

"Where's my bag, boy? I had a bag of stuff." He looked at me, sudden, malevolent. Panicked, wild-eyed, angry, he accused me, "Where's my stuff?"

"It's in the cabin." I pointed back to the cabin. "I didn't touch it."

He jumped up and ran as best he could to the cabin while I followed. He looked around. Not seeing the bag at first. "On the floor, the bunk room." I pointed to the other room. He snatched up the bag, felt it without opening it. I could see the wave of calm pass over his body, a smile on his face half-formed. He opened the bag and took out a full bottle of something clear. "Whew, had a little scare there." His canteen was there too, he shook it and took the cap off and sniffed it and smiled with approval.

The old man paused and looked around the room. "Say's where your 'frigerator?" He looked around some more and fixed his eyes on the lantern. "Got no lights. Got no TV. What kinda place you got here?"

"It's not mine. We're in the woods. We ... I was hitchhiking. You were in the back. The driver turned off the main road. You peed in his bed. He kicked you out, kicked me out too. It was raining so we came in here."

He looked at me uncomprehending. Then stopped and listened. "Don't hear no cars. Don't hear nothing. Where are we?"

"You don't remember?" It was all very strange. He'd seen all this the night before.

A flash of recognition crossed his face. "WooWee," a world-weary sigh of lament rather than one of enthusiasm. "You a drinker?" He looked at me up and down. "Here we got a case of blackout.

"Blackout. Blackout happens with us sportin' men. Sportin' man starts the night in one place. 'Oops,' he's someplace else. Don't know how he gets there. There he is. Where he is? Who knows how? I was in this bar, chatting up this lady. Now I'm here."

"Last night you were fine. I mean, you were drunk, but you weren't passed out or anything, not till the end, and I guess in the truck, but you weren't passed out, blacked out, whatever you call it. We were walking around and talking. We came here."

"See boy. Boy, that's the funny thing about it. Blackout ain't passing out. People tell me what I been doing. Drove to Dakota, don't remember nothing. Nothing in the old brain sticks. Ain't passed out, that's a different thing. People tell me I'm just like normal,

normal drunk. Don't remember. Like taking a book and ripping out a page. Page just gone. Gone, don't know where it's gone."

The idea of it seemed strange to me. I didn't believe him. I'd never heard of a blackout before. He tried to explain. "Ok boy, one year ago today. Right this minute. What was you doing?"

I didn't remember. I had been in school. "At class," I guessed.

"What class?"

"I didn't know." I tried to remember my schedule, but the actual class, that was gone.

"See boy, you don't remember. What you was wearing? What ya had for breakfast? Who you was talking to? Talking to your mom? Being with your girly friend? Talking on the phone? What ya had for lunch? Same thing, 'cept I can't remember last night. Gotta figure it out."

Was he right? I tried to remember even lunch a month ago. A cheeseburger with swiss? A wild guess, but the actual act of eating was gone, not remembered. And with my girlfriend, how many times had we made love? I remember the first time she spoke French, maybe a few times after that, but not them all, they ran together. But I could remember the last time. Damn. It all seemed odd. Not remembering even the night before, just a few hours past. He was drunk, but not so bad, not crazy, incoherent drunk, not falling down, puking drunk. We'd walked on the road. Talked. Had a conversation. Ran from the storm. How could he not remember it? How many drinks did *I* have? Did I remember each one? I tried to puzzle it out.

"Let's do a little adventuring," he said while I was still puzzling. One day, in later years, I'd wake up and remember him—but not the night before—and understand the whole business of blackout. Meanwhile, he was up, lit-up, ready for life.

"See what we got here. Keep your eyes open. See what providence provides."

He went out the door, and I followed. The sun was above the trees, the low-angle, amber-morning light had given way white daylight. Vapor was curling off the corrugated metal roof of the big building. The rain had left us a hot day, an early summer day while the calendar was barely spring. We'd found quite a place in this idyllic camp on the lake. The piles of trash on the road had kept the vandals away. So it was just time and rain and sun and nature making their slow progress back to paradise. I supposed it had been some gentleman's hunting camp decades ago, a place to get away and fish and shoot and smoke cigars. It had been built with care and was still strong. Dozens of pines had sprung up in what had been the clearing, but the sandy soil, and the trees themselves, had kept out the undergrowth. And the dogs, and perhaps deer too, had left a tangle of paths for us to follow.

The big building had two sets of oversized doors that opened on the lake. From the way it was situated and from ages-old tracks in the ground, I decided it had been a boathouse. There was a side door away from the lake and some shuttered windows. One of the boards was loose and falling away. The old man gave it a tug and tried to peer inside. "Too dark. Dark in there," he said. He gave it a harder tug and leaned down to look.

"The dogs," I reminded him. "I wouldn't stick my head in there."

The old man stepped back, "Let's try them big doors."

One of the big doors had mostly broken free of its top hinge and was ajar. I was wary. It was the crack where the puppies had emerged. I figured that there must be big-dog entrance and exit around the back—by the collapsed corner probably. The old man pulled at the door, and the bottom hinge gave way, and the door crashed on the ground. The sun reached into the darkness. He took a step and sniffed the air. "Guess youse right about them dogs." He looked down. The ground was muddy and held prints of their paws. I didn't see any pooches. But there were plenty of nooks and such for them to hide. "Wait," I said. He paused. I went over to the firepit and picked up two hefty sticks. I handed one to him. He gave a nod and smiled toward me. We were a team.

In the shadow of my memory I've done my best to reconstruct what happened over those few days. What the old drunk said, and what I said. What happened. How I felt. What I learned. At that moment, when we went into the light and the dark of the abandoned boathouse, it was still a wonderful adventure, the kind of experience I had taken to the road to discover. It was a long time ago, and my memories are colored by my life, but some moments remain clear and timeless. And I know that I am always that young man, and I am always that old man, and I am always the man that I am now. And as much as I can hold that any memory is true, what I clearly, truly, remember about the moment is that we two were one.

I guess that's why I stayed with him when it got bad. I could have just shouldered my pack and walked out. But it would have been as like to abandon myself.

Thus we went into the glare of the sun and the shadow of the corners with our foolish sticks and our timeless bond and our human curiosity. In retrospect I don't know why we even went in there. We could have just left well enough alone and kept to our little cabin. For that matter, we could have just left. The old man still had booze enough in him to function. We should have just gone out to the road and started walking. We would have gotten somewhere eventually, gotten a ride, found a main road. But we didn't.

The place stunk of dogs. Stray hairs floated in the sunlight, more hair where the sun was on the dirt floor. It smelled too of wet dirt and rotten wood. They'd left the boats. There was a wooden skiff that was just the right size for our lake. It'd been stored overturned on a couple of sawhorses, but the sawhorses had collapsed, and the boat was bottom-up on the ground. It seemed like a good place for dogs to hide, so I gave the bottom a couple of solid thunks with my stick. A few flecks of paint came off, and I could see that the seams had opened up over the years. There was an old sailboat too, a scow. It didn't look too bad. They'd left it on blocks, so the hull hadn't touched the damp earth. It was mostly just dirty as far as I could tell. Off to the right were a couple of upside-down canoes, a canvas one torn to shreds and Grumman aluminum. It was banged up a bit, but looked serviceable. There was a little tunnel leading under the Grumman. I stepped over to it with my stick raised and gave the canoe a kick. Nothing. No dogs. I lifted the canoe up, the dogs had definitely made a little nest for themselves underneath, but they were gone.

The old man was checking out a tool bench on the opposite wall, picking up rusty wrenches and such and putting them down one by one. He moved over to a fifty-gallon drum, reached in, pulled up a bottle and held it to the light. He rolled it around, looked closely, pulled the cork, gave it a sniff. Up to his lips and whatever was in it drained into his throat. He coughed once, then smiled at me, "Somebody wasting some good whiskey." He took every opportunity to satisfy himself without hesitation. He had a good eye for opportunity and an amazing knack for finding booze. He started reaching in the drum and pulling stuff out. He threw papers and cans on the dirt and took whatever bottles he found and carefully put them on the workbench. He pulled out a paper Japanese lantern, let it unfold into a ball, held it in the sun. The colors were still bright after all these years. "Somebody having a party, party in the pines." There were more lanterns and some paper streamers in cellophane packages. He took one and threw it. The bright paper rolled off his hand through the dark and into the light like it had a life of its own, then fell limp to the dirt. He tossed me a pack. I held an end and threw a coil, and it too rolled through space into a shaft of sunlight. A party it was. He pulled a few more bottles out of the drum and announced, "I think we got a sporting man. Man here liked to drink."

He stood back and looked at his bottle collection. It was mostly empty whiskey bottles, but one had a couple of sips in it. There was one with some green liquid, like the one in the cabinet, and another with an oval shape that had something clear in it. "We got us a nice little bar here boy. We'll save the liqueurs for dessert."

As my eyes adjusted to the dark I could pick out details in the shadows. Paddles for the canoes leaning against the wall and boat cushions hanging from pegs. Oars for the skiff. What looked like a mast and boom on a rack. A rake, a couple of long-handled shovels, an axe, fishing rods in a corner, a pile of canvas and rag. Sails? The old man was moving toward the back door. There was another room. He grabbed the doorknob and gave it a tug, but the structure had shifted over the years just enough to jam the door. He gave it another hard pull. For a moment I feared the jammed door might be the only thing holding up the roof. Another hard yank and the doorknob came off in his hand. He fell back on the ground. No surprise there. He wasn't real steady on his feet even in the best of circumstances. I grabbed the axe from the corner and went over to the door. Still on his back the old man cried out, "There you go, son. That's the idea. Bash that sucker in."

A few good swings and we were in. "What we got here? Can't see a damn thing." I could just make out that the room was stacked with wooden crates and cardboard boxes. The cardboard had rotted and spilled cans onto the floor. The old man picked up a wooden crate and carried it outside. I did the same. By the time I got into the light the he was already crowing about our discovery. "We got us a smorgasbord. We got us a jackpot. Jackpot we got!" The crate read, *Ration–10 in 1.*

"C-Rats," he said excitedly. "C-Rats. We ain't gonna starve now." He yanked at the rusted metal straps holding his crate together.

"Got some familiarity with these," he said shaking an olive-drab can. "Coffee. Coffee and sugar and smokes.

"Read this for me."

"*Bread Type Unit.*"

"Read 'em all."

"*Sliced Bacon. Beef and Vegetables. Pork Sausage Links. Meat and Beans.*"

The old man greedily dug into our treasure—cereal, honey, raisins, powdered eggs, evaporated milk, caramels, and a big can of coffee. "Smokes." He held up a pack that read, *Lucky Strikes.*

"What ya got in yours?" he said motioning to the crate I had carried out. I pulled it open. It held small boxes labeled—*Breakfast, Dinner, Supper.* They were field rations. He seemed to know all about them. I tore a breakfast box open—crackers, coffee and cigarettes, gum, sugar, water purification tables. The main course was a small, flat can— *Chopped Ham and Egg.* You opened it with a little key that fit into a slot on the side of the can and peeled off a layer of metal to pop the top off, just like the coffee can. There was even a flat, wooden spoon.

"All them boxes in there," the old man said. "We got us some eatin'.

"We'll make us a mulligan. Hobo stew boy. Ain't so bad when you're hungry."

I wasn't so sure. Ptomaine in the middle of nowhere didn't seem like a very good idea.

I pulled out a tiny packet of toilet paper, a thoughtful addition that looked wholly inadequate to the cuisine.

"This is thirty years old, at least."

"Mission gourmet," he said going to work on *Meat and Beans*. I unpeeled the *Chopped Ham and Egg* tin.

It didn't smell like death, more like dog food. The old man's can seemed to be chunks of maybe beans and maybe meat in a thick, maybe gravy. We were both looking at our meals, thinking about taking a bite, and for all his enthusiasm, the reality of the contents of the can gave even him pause for thought.

"Maybe we should try it on the dogs," he said.

It seemed cruel to me. But we left the question hanging as the old man began digging through a collection of big cans that I had gathered up in my arms and set before him. "You did good, son. Good stuff here. Here's all we need for a nice little time." He held up a can, *Fruit Cocktail*, and with a wry smile said, "Party time. Time to party. We got some cocktails here."

"That's not what you think," I pedantically explained to him. "It's not a cocktail. It's not a drink. It's just fruit and syrup."

The old man gave me a look of great compassion, sighed, and went on to ask if there were more cans of *Fruit Cocktail*.

He felt on the bottom of the can for the key and put in the tab and opened it. He gave it a tentative sniff.

"It's not a cocktail," I said. "It's not a drink." He was getting stupid on me.

He took a sip and rolled it around in his mouth.

"It's not really a cocktail. Not like that," I said.

"How much of this stuff in there?"

"Cases."

I remember him looking up and smiling at me. A superior smile, he knew something I didn't. He may have been a drunken drunk, but as I was to learn, he wasn't stupid. A stupid boozer wouldn't have lasted as long as he had.

He took another little sip and handed me the can. "Smell ok to you?"

"It smells like fruit and sugar. Look, we shouldn't eat this stuff. It's expired. It's like botulism or something. It'll kill you."

"Nice bouquet," he said, ignoring my concern and confusion.

I thought he was going mad. "It's not a cocktail!"

"Not yet it ain't. But it's gonna be.

"How much of them sugar things we got?"

"A lot."

"See how many boxes of that fruit we got. And sugar, we need lots of sugar."

He smiled and laughed and might have even actually licked his lips. "Gonna make some wine son. Opening a winery in the pinery."

"Winery in the pinery." I had to laugh, crazy, old coot. "What the hell."

Evidently we had the makings of a first-class batch of backwoods booze.

When I was much younger, child of memories dreamlike and half-remembered, I had a playmate whose maternal grandparents had a farm. At least it had been a farm, but was more like a house in the country when I knew it. I think his grandparents had farmed the ground at one time, but by my time they rented most of the fields and kept a few chickens. I remember hunting for eggs in the hidden nests of semi-feral hens and a dull red tractor in a barn, and I remember that they made their own wine.

There is a mystical ritual preserved in my mind of these grandparents with thick accents. I remember a cool corner of a dirt-floored cellar, and I conjure up vaguely-realized, dark casks and dirty bottles with necks exposed. I recall Grampa's broken promise that I should someday return in the fall for the picking and crushing and bottling. Mostly I remember the wine bottles taken out with great reverence before the noontime meal, glasses all around and a small glass mixed with water for each of us children. It was a friend's family, with all their own personal rituals that I didn't fully understand, but amazed and delighted me. Then, I don't know why, my memory ends. I stopped going there? My playmate gone, a mysterious disappearance from childhood I never quite understood. Maybe Grampa died or they sold the farm or my playmate's family moved away or ... I don't know. It was just all gone.

That the old drunk and I would, ourselves, make wine from the army rations seemed sacrilegious, but there was also something wild and forbidden, as if I had discovered in this old man some oracle of esoteric knowledge where a mystery of my past caught my present. We were going to make booze—Bathtub Gin, Moonshine, White Lightning, Nectar of the Gods, Chain Lightning, Happy Sally, The Preacher's Lye, Kick in the Ass, Skull Cracker, the Balm of Gilead. Even in my naïveté I could see that what we were making wasn't exactly wine or gin or whiskey or anything that you'd drink by choice. It wasn't anything except something that would carry an alcohol content that would get you a little drunk if you held your nose and drank enough of it. And the esoteric knowledge wasn't anything that any Joe who had spent a bit of time behind bars or in an army boot camp or on a ship at sea hadn't learned. But it was all new to me, and it was exciting.

It actually isn't much of a big deal to make booze. Nature does the work. All you need is something that will ferment, which is just another way of saying that it spoils. When sugar, in pretty much anything, spoils it breaks down into carbon dioxide and alcohol. You bleed the carbon dioxide off into the atmosphere, the alcohol goes into you. And if all goes well, you get drunk. The old man's plan was to take all the *Fruit Cocktail* cans and mix them up with all the sugar and put the whole mess out in the sun. The heat would help it along, and we'd have enough booze to last us a couple of weeks.

My job was to dig through the rubbish in the boathouse, get the biggest bottles I could find. "Make sure they got nothing good in 'em. Wash 'em out good." The old man would carry the fruit cocktail and sugar to the firepit, which would be our laboratory, and fill the bottles, which would be our fermentation chambers. I carried out an armful of gallon-sized empties. "See if you can find a funnel," he yelled to me. It was good to see he was thinking this through.

"Wash them things out," the old man commanded again. Why not? I didn't mind. It was all part of the adventure. I washed the big bottles found in the boathouse, then went behind the building to the camp's rubbish pile to find more. It really was rubbish —rusted cans and broken glass, an old bike without a front wheel, pieces from an outboard, a cylinder head someone had taken an ax to, a busted metal bed frame, scraps of rotten mattress with gray stuffing coming out, forgotten things that had once been someone's joy. All I was hoping for was some more gallon jugs or big jars or something, but found none. Any big glass was broken. Tucked under a wet clump of mattress stuffing was a bottle of whiskey. I saw as I pulled it out that it was a full bottle, still sealed. I almost called out to alert the old man and bring him my prize, but thought better of it. Something held me back. And I hid it again and put the bottle out of my mind for the time being. Maybe I didn't want to stop the adventure of the winemaking. Or maybe I was keeping a little insurance for myself. In any case, the old man was yelling something at me. He was trying to put the fruit cocktail into the empty jugs, making a mess of it. He tried to pour it in, but the neck opening was too small, the chunks of fruit jammed, the syrup ran over his hand. It was obvious that it wasn't going to work, but the old man had to try. Maybe there was a funnel in the boathouse? I'd look. Everything else we'd wanted seemed to be at hand when we needed it. But I didn't see a funnel. He had a low tolerance for frustration and was soon silhouetted in the door of the boathouse demanding the funnel, which we didn't have. He tore around the room looking for what didn't exist. Or maybe what did exist, and he, we, couldn't see. Then he stopped. He stood still for a moment. And I could almost see him change his mental gears, letting one idea go and switching to another. Filling jugs was out. We were going big-time.

"Mass production boy, all the marbles in one barrel, ducks in a row, all the duckets in a single bucket. Help me empty this thing out." And he was turning over the fifty-gallon drum and emptying out all the bottles and broken trash. He was pretty rough with it, and when the two of us upended it glass broke. "Shit." The old man looked down. One of the bottles had had something in it. Actually it looked as if it had been pretty full, maybe it was water, but the old man got down on his knees and sniffed it, and I thought for a minute he was going to eat the dirt that had soaked it up. But he didn't, just pronounced with authority, "This man was an alki. Alki's hide bottles. We gotta keep a sharp eye. Yes sir! This man was a alki."

We dragged the drum over to the lake and washed it best we could, scrubbing with sand and lake water. I mentioned that there was soap with the rations. I could get some. "Ruin the bouquet," said in all seriousness. Then, "Gotta be in the sun. Gotta stay warm." He was the high priest of fermentation magic. I didn't know it at the time, but there was a bit more to the magic than the old man was remembering. We needed yeast to get the fermentation process started. There should have been enough naturally-occurring yeast floating around in the air to make it work, particularly out in the woods in the spring, that's how people got wine from grapes and beer from hops before chemists figured out the role of yeast—there are usually a few yeast spores floating around to get the fermentation process going. But with those minute amounts of random yeast, fermentation could take weeks. We didn't have that kind of time. Today, wine connoisseurs and beer aficionados will simply add some commercial yeast to speed things up. A beer-brewing buddy I once kept company with informed me that before anyone knew about yeast, brewers had special sticks that they'd use to stir the mash. The sticks were thought to be magic, but really were just infused with yeast spores that would be transferred from batch to batch to speed the fermentation process. "They fought wars over those sticks," he solemnly told me over a thick, bitter, raspberry concoction he'd made in his basement and called beer. In prisons and on army bases and aboard navy ships and God only knows where else, sans magic stick or brewer's yeast, baker's yeast would do. Or simply a slice or two of bread would supply the required magic. Tragically, a magic we did not possess.

Thus, our little winemaking was doomed from the start. All it actually held was the illusion of a dozen gallons of bliss for the old man, a hollow promise as it turned out, but one that would keep him in our little Paradise Found past the point of prudence, until there really was no more booze. But neither of us knew it at the time, and we continued with enthusiasm.

The old man put a stick in the ground and made a theatrically thorough study of exactly where the drum-warming sun would or would not shine, and we dragged the drum over to the appropriate location. He was quite pleased with himself that he'd thought to place to drum before we filled it. "Gonna be heavy," he explained. So we filled our hopes with fruit cocktail and sugar, and the old man reached in and over the top of the drum and stirred with his arm. Some vague memory informed him that we needed to keep the air out, so he covered the drum with a piece of canvas from the boathouse.

I guessed from the winemaking that we weren't leaving anytime soon. I might as well settle in. And why not? This was a nice little adventure. No hurry to go on. I had half a pack of smokes in my pocket and another stashed in my pack. If I conserved them, kept them from the old man, we could hang out here for a few days. I had a sack of granola, a couple of *Tiger's Milk Bars*. We had lots of coffee and rations, extra smokes if we got desperate enough. There must be fish in the lake. Maybe I could trap some rabbits like the old man had said the night before? And the old man? Must be good for a story or two. It wasn't the jazz and bars and romance of Montréal, but still, it was an adventure—like Jack and Gary in the mountains, or Jack's lonely summer on Desolation Peak. That was my whole point, right?

I went out and sat down by the firepit and looked my the lake. The idea of staying changed my perspective. I took possession, turned and looked at my new Eden—trees, lake, cabin, boathouse, firepit— my summer camp, my vacation idyll, my spring break destination. I laughed. My classmates were planning real vacations in Daytona, Biloxi, Paris. Or they were working double shifts to scrape some much needed cash together. They had papers to write, exams to make up, dope to smoke, beers to drink, lovers to love, jobs accepted, careers planned, linen-paper-printed résumés, goals, graduate schools, fiancés, marriages, children, mortgages, stock portfolios, taxes, retirement plans, grandchildren, family crypts, epitaphs purposely cut in granite—lives laid out in good sense. I had only some mythical idea over the next hill, an idea—I didn't even know what—beyond some dense stand of pines and across the impossible swamp.

In two months my days of schooling would be over.

Impatient, I couldn't wait. Or maybe I couldn't stand for those days of my youth to end.

Monday morning I sleep through class. Wake late, hung-over, don't care a second more about John Updike's smug, upside-down beer can or the "chill of death" in E.B. White's groin. Aspirin and coffee and I fill my pack, strap on my down bag, tuck two twenty-dollar bills in my shoe. The *Road* is all the education I need. The plan is to head north, up to Canada, across the top of Superior and then Montréal. A buddy's older brother has gone there to beat the draft—buddy says that the brother says there is a jazz scene. They speak French. That's all it takes. I stuff my *Rand McNally* in a side pocket and stick out my thumb. Impatient, impetuous, idealistic—I want to find *It* right then—the *It* that Jack was searching out. I want to be *there,* to be with Jack and the sweet port and the jazz and the girls. I want to know Avalokiteśvara, Jack's bodhisattva, who stands beside me, listening, looking, jamming with the rest, digging the beat of compassion. I want to be with Neal yelling, "Go. Go. Blow, baby, blow," while some horn man's solo lifts us out of the world into what?—I don't know. I want to be with the poets making history, shouting obscenities to the masses, "slugging a glug" on the gallon of Burgundy. Bellowing, I want to sit on the edge of the stage with Jack yelling, "Go, Go, Go," while Ginsberg reads his great poem, run wild in the night with Zen Lunatics, eat with chopsticks, hop boulder-to-boulder on the mystical mountain, make love to a beautiful woman who cooks me flapjacks in morning. I want to ride hell-bent on the back of some flatboard truck into the desert. Get desperately drunk. Stumble. Piss into the night. Get back up again and again. I want to climb the Mountain of Desolation, meditate in solitude with clouds below, dawn above, sit on the door-open shitter with the peaks at my feet—fierce, sublime beauty—chipmunks snack on my oatmeal. And *my* poem inscribed on the living rock of eternity, now sitting quiet to satori.

I looked out at my lake. It was my Adventure, and my heart was glad.

# a sporting man

I'd fallen asleep in the sand. The old man had gone to the cabin and his bunk. I had simply settled down on my back to look at the clouds, not intending to sleep, but woke as the sun was setting. For a few wonderful moments our rustic camp was cut through with red-infused rays. Before it got too dark, I'd make a mulligan. The name had stuck in my head. I pulled out rations marked *Stew—Beef and Vegetable, Pork, Ham, Beans and Franks,* and emptied the cans into a big pot and kindled a fire. I filled the kettle with lake water, poured a bit into the pot to thin out the mulligan, and boiled the rest for coffee. I made my hobo joe like before, throwing a few handfuls of ground coffee into the boiling kettle. We had nice ceramic mugs in the cabin, but I chose an empty ration can for a hobo cup. I couldn't hold my makeshift cup, too hot, so I wrapped my bandana around it for insulation. To complete the picture I hazarded a cigarette from the rations. The rustle of feral dogs in the woods added to the romance.

Scruffy Terror watched from the underbrush. I tossed over a mostly-empty can. The mutt grabbed it and fled. I thought about what the old man had said about testing the food on the pooches. I figured if I cooked it long enough I'd kill anything toxic. We were lucky. At least I was, it might have been easier on the old man if he'd just eaten some poison soup right then and there. But here I was living the hobo life. The cigarette was stale and terrible, the coffee burnt and acidic, the stew smelled like I was cooking old shoes. (And I didn't have much faith that it would taste any better than it smelled.) Still, an idyllic interlude. My Adventure.

Then he was banging around in the cabin, awake from his afternoon nap. He was talking up a storm, laughing, all at once. Did he have someone else in there with him? I knew he didn't. A new man appeared at the door. Clean. He wore a crisp, red, button-up shirt. He'd replaced his pee-stained khakis with a pair of canvas bush pants. A regular Paul Bunyan. His hair was slicked back, newly combed and held tight with natural grease. It was the old man, redressed and rejuvenated. He held up a foot, a tooled cowboy boot on it. Best of all, a fresh bottle of booze held out in his hand. "In the boot," he said holding up the bottle. "Some nice man left it here in this nice boot. Left me some nice clothes too. Damn nice of him." He wore the singular smile of a drunkard anticipating his next drunk. But first he wanted coffee. I poured him a ration can full and held it out. He looked at me sadly and shook his head, got up without a word and went back to the cabin and returned with a nice ceramic mug. I poured, and he waved me off with shaking hand at half cup. He wanted a cigarette. I offered him one from the rations pack. He reached in his pocket and took out one of his own. He leaned over the mulligan and took a sniff and gave a big sigh, not sharing particularly in my romance of the open road.

The cherry on the cigarette danced at the end of his fingers. He sipped the hot coffee carefully, holding the mug with two hands as he brought it to his lips while he contemplated the fifty-gallon drum.

"We use all the sugar?"

"We used a lot."

"Coffee could use some."

We sat in quiet for a time. Cold was coming up from the ground and off the lake, the heat of the day escaping into the twilight. "S'posed to keep it warm," he said after a while. I knew he was talking about the drum. He got up and walked over to it and around it and put his hand on it.

"You hungry?" I motioned to the pot.

"Naw."

We had another cup of coffee and more cigarettes. While darkness descended we sat before the fire and watched the smoke swirl and the lake turn into a black void. Surrounded by night and the creatures therein, a small circle of illumination became our world.

"Gotta keep it warm."

"Maybe wrap with a blanket or something?"

"Treat it like a baby."

He was looking at the drum.

"Maybe we should build a fire around it? That'd warm it up quick," I suggested.

"Naw. Make 'er too hot. Just wants to be warm. Got to fur-ment. Warm it up with a couple of them bricks 'round the fire maybe."

It was no simple matter to carry the hot bricks without gloves, but we did it. Teamwork. With two long, straight branches and the bricks carried like stretcher-born casualties we made a circle around the drum. Then we wrapped it with two blankets from the cabin, and the old man was happy,

"Time to splice the main brace."

I had no idea what he was talking about.

He walked over to the cabin. I heard a few bangs and bumps and saw the flare of a match and glow of the lantern and the old man silhouetted in the door with two glasses.

"You got any ice?" he said.

What was he getting at? Was he crazy? In a blackout thinking he was someplace else, someplace that had ice?

"Splash of soda?" he asked. "Maybe we can rustle us up a couple of them little paper umbrellas, 'long with them paper lanterns in the shed?"

I could see he was smiling, joking. I hadn't been sure. I nodded no, smiled back. He was a happy drunk.

"Taking mine neat," he said. "Two fingers?" He put about a shot and a half in a glass and handed it to me, then poured about the same for himself.

He took a soft, careful sip. Another soft sip, waited a moment to be sure it was staying down, then drank the rest in a single swallow. I sipped mine. He poured himself more and took a good-sized jolt.

He stuck out his hand suddenly. "Harry. Name's Harry. Good to meet you."

"That's my name!"

"Whose name?"

"My name."

"Your name?"

"Me. Harry. That's my name too. I'm Harry too."

The old man took it all in stride. I took his still outstretched hand and shook it.

"Pleased to meet you, Harry. Hope we don't get confused," Harry said with a broad smile. The booze was taking effect. His future, the fifty-gallon drum of fermentation, was safely bubbling away. He was on an island of safety. I knew how he felt. I was the same hitching. When I got a long, comfortable ride, I could sit back and know I had two or four or whatever hours of comfort and motion. For Harry it was booze and warmth and the promise of more booze. That doomed dream, the fifty-gallon drum of hope, made all the difference. And the new bottle was still half full.

"So now, Harry? What exactly brings you this tiny abode here?"

"Busted. Looking for work. Cousin's got a gas station in Baltimore," I replied in my ungrammatical, on-the-road talk. "Said he'd give me a job. Headed there. Busted. Ain't got a dime. Said he'd help me out."

That was my story. I was hitchhiking because I was broke. I was looking for work, headed toward an imaginary cousin who would employ me at the illusionary gas station that lay in the direction of wherever I was going. Telling people that I was a college student on a Kerouacish lark didn't seem to be a proper kind of story. Sometimes I half-believed me myself, but in the back of my head knew that there was a dime in my jeans and a phone number in my memory and parents at my home who would accept a collect call and wire whatever cash to wherever I was. Funny thing is, years later when I look back at those days, I see the germ of something already in me. My friends didn't capriciously stick out their thumbs and hitchhike across the country. And I guess I didn't do it without cause either, but what it was that was driving me was stronger and darker and more destructive than anything I would have believed at the time.

"Gas station in Balt-tee-moore?" the old man queried. "I've been to Baltimore. Where's this gas station at?"

I'd told the story dozens of times, nobody ever asked me where, specifically, before. I had no idea. "Main Street."

"East or West ... *Main* Street?"

"East?"

"What brand?

"Gulf?

"Sinclair?

"Tex-E-co?"

He threw the questions out so fast I didn't have time to think.

"Your cousin's got a name?" he asked with a smile. And before I could answer, answered himself.

"Maybe named Harry?" he said with a chuckle. The old man wasn't buying it.

"My name really is Harry," I said. "You want to see my student ID?"

Harry laughed aloud, "Naw. Don't care if you don't want to tell me your business."

He was too perceptive to believe my lie about the job, too experienced to push me for the truth, too wise to think the truth really mattered. He just wanted to know if I was a threat or not.

"It's okay boy. No need to be pouting. Got us a nice little berth.

"Might's as well enjoy. Have a drink."

Harry was a pro at getting by. That's how he survived. People liked him. He wasn't scary. He was a nice man fallen on hard times. Friendly, he could read people. He saw that he'd pushed me a bit too hard, and he backed off. After all, I was all he had. He might as well make the best.

He had, or so I thought at the time, come to accept his lot in life. When he was drunk, smiling, well-dressed, his life didn't look so bad. I would come to understand that there is an appealing purity to a drunken existence—a clearly defined goal and an immediate gratification, an intensity of pure, bestial satisfaction when the bottle is found and full. And as the bottle empties, a joyous freedom at my lack of responsibility to anyone or anything but the booze. I remember myself looking at a half-drunk fifth and smiling and thinking that I was too drunk to do anything. Absolved of all responsibility and still with half a bottle—I was free.

Not a bad life. Until it's not.

"Whew. I gotta take a wizzzz." Harry stood, not a touch unsteadily, and wandered into the woods to pee.

"What about you?" I called out to him. "What's your story? Where you headed?"

"Bottle Baby." Harry called out as he walked back zipping up his fly. I noticed as he closed on the fire that he'd dribbled urine on his new pants.

"Born to the bottle.

"Whiskey's fifth.

"Never had no mama's tit.

"I was born to the bottle.

"Jus' a sporting man.

"Doing best I can.

"Here. There.

"Don't matter no where.

"Jus' take her as she comes.

"And ah one day.

"One day's youse done."

He was happy to have an appreciative audience. We were going to celebrate a bit, ration the booze, just enough tonight to catch a buzz and a good night's sleep, keep our supply going until the drum was ready, keep the vacation going until, well—we'd worry about that later. He was a drunk. That's how he thought. I was young, didn't really know yet.

"Bottle born.

"Bottle bred.

"Bottle's my bed."

He took a swig from the fifth. Glasses now forgotten. He handed it to me. I'd had enough to want more, and I took a big gulp, swallowed and once again tipped the bottle high and filled my mouth and opened my throat and felt the burning salvation flow into me. His eyes met mine as I handed the bottle back. And I thought I saw pity in them. I didn't understand then, but he'd seen my thirst. I can still remember his beautiful eyes and the way he looked at me and my sudden realization as I remembered that look many years later, understanding finally what this Harry had seen in me. But I kept on drinking then as I did that night. Because this wasn't the night for the horrors of my tomorrow. This was the night for the bravado of the fresh bottle and the beautiful road.

"That's good whiskey," he said. "Bottle fed. Whiskey bred. Born to drink. I was jus' born to drink."

He took another swig and offered it to me. I took a careful sip this time, handed it back and avoided his eyes.

"Bottle fed. Whiskey's dead. Ain't an inch of difference."

Bravado, the first flush of relief, a fresh bottle doing its work. He perked up and started rhapsodizing. I try now not to romanticize him. He wasn't a prophet. Not an oracle, nor philosopher. Not a poet. No saint. Not even a sinner. He was just a drunken man stumbling from one day to the next.

"Harry, you can't just go through life drinking all the time."

"Why not?"

"I mean ..."

"Hell. I'm doing it!"

I listened in awe to the years of accumulated clichés—the accumulated wisdom of not just Harry, but the collective wisdom of a thousand barrooms. And for me, the first time hearing them, I thought they were original thoughts, Harry's genius applied to life. He'd spent a lifetime caging drinks and had figured out what worked and what didn't, what tale got someone to nod in agreement and would build a bond that led to a free drink. If he hadn't stumbled onto Chicago's Madison Street, he would have been a natural for the Avenue in Manhattan. I don't think there was anything sly or manipulative in what he said. It was just the way he was. I don't know that he consciously thought it through to a drink. Perhaps he just wanted to please whomever he was sitting next to.

"Spent three days in Needles. Needles, California. US 40. Arizona state line. Three days trying to git out. Never forget. Same cops rolling by, shift after shit, giving me a wave and smile. Smiling, laughing at me still being there. Shift after shit," and he laughed at his joke. "Jail without bars, boy. Worst kinda jail, no bars, no booze. Get it? Jail with no bars? No bars, boy.

"Young I was, jus' like you. Now I know better. Better give it up. Take a bus when the rides ain't coming. Times ya can't do nothing but wait, but sometimes ya take a bus. Trick is to know when. When to hold and when to fold. Ya gotta flow with the road. Lean into them curves. HIT THEM BRAKES! BATTEN DOWN THEM HATCHES! Tie 'er down tight and ride 'er out. Sometimes ya run with the wind. Sometimes ya heave-to and ride her out, take it on the nose," and he laughed hard and loud. "Thar she blows.

"Hole up and hide. Sleep when you're tired. Eat when you're hungry. Drink whenever ya can! That's my philosophy."

He poured himself another drink. He was getting fired up now. His manner reminded me of a college professor--a guy who taught the English poets, loved Coleridge--and it occurred to me, maybe the professor was drunk too. He got fired up the same way, and of course Coleridge—God only knows what he was on.

"Son. Let me tell ya 'bout the road. Santa Barbara south, the bay and the pier, there's strip of Mexican places. Big, cold pitchers of beer and big, hot plates of beans and rice and enchiladas stuffed with stuff you don't want to know what it is. Union Pacific rolls right down the coast. Pretty as the Rockies in the spring. Take ya where ya got to go. Nobody bothers with ya. Sleep on the beach, make yourself a quiet, little fire, eat a can of beans, nobody rousts ya. People's friendly, guess 'coz it's warm and all. All year 'round. Go there. Don't never leave. Whew, California, too many bums. Bums too many. Something in the air sucks a man's soul.

"Now Chicago, son she ain't no lady. Don't go near her. No way in and no way out. Six-lane highways coming and going and nobody going nowhere most the time. And they got suburbs and suburbs and suburbs with suburb cops got nothing to do but watch ya walking. That's all they do, won't arrest ya and take in, won't give ya a lift. They just cruise along behind and make ya keep walking and walking and walking. Man just wants to sit sometimes. Sometimes ain't no place for a sporting man to sit. Keep ya walking, walking and walking. Coming down from Wisconsin, trying to catch 80, she's a devil. Get a ride straight through, that's my advice, get a ride straight through. Ask if they's going to Gary. Gotta get to Gary. Gary, Indiana. Loop ain't so bad. Nice ladies in fur coats, warm pockets, folding money in them pockets. Help a man out. But don't be there in the winter. Winter ain't no time to be in the Loop.

"Minneapolis, she's a town. Madison, Ann Arbor. College boys, college girls, buy ya beer, listen to stories. Salt of the earth. Help a man out. Buy a beer, buy a sandwich. Not in winter. Don't go in winter. Had a buddy, drunk one afternoon, stepped out to take a pee, fell down and froze himself. Dead. Cut off his toes. They cut off his toes, not a bad ways to go. How'd ya bury a man with no toes? Don't ya know? Austin's alright. Good in the winter. Lots of good folk. But some bad ones too, real bad cowboys, boys wearing boots.

"New Orleans? Sporting man's paradise? Damn bunch of drunks. Too many. Too many hands holding out nothing, holding out for change. Hot. Stinking. Bed bugs and lice and stink and fleas. Ain't no winter to kill the fleas. No winter to kill the weak. Florida too.

Hell, I'd rather freeze myself. In cold, people who's warm will feel bad for ya. In the heat, heat on the street, North Beach, they just feel bad for themselves and don't give ya nothing."

The stories went on, towns known and towns unknown, and towns I would someday know. There were the roads too—roads and highways with names that would die with the last of the 'bos—the Mother Road, the Hillbilly Highway, the Lincoln Highway from Central Park West to the Golden Gate and every town in between. The Dixie Highway—U.S. 25—from dead south to Detroit, hard-working people looking for a better life, back and forth, up and down, heading north with nothing but dust in your pocket, back south in a shiny, new Ford of your own. Old US 70—the Broadway of America—coast to coast with the promise of the Pacific, the Middle Way, not too hot not too cold, a good highway till the interstates took it over and stole its number and changed its route so that only one old trucker in Kansas even remembered it and told me it had a name. I knew for myself the Pacific Coast Highway, a stunning trip, hard to hitch, where Kerouac famously got stuck and went mad with the DTs.

Once it gets into you, you can't get it out. I remember walking through peaceful neighborhoods on the edge of Chicago—hundreds of modest homes, closely packed but snugly private. It was dusk in the summer, and I could see into the houses through screened, front porch doors and opened widows, families eating supper, watching the television, sitting at tables playing cards, laughing, being together. I wondered how they did it. I felt contempt and envy at the same time. I wanted to sit with them and be happy to just sit. Me, tired and dirty with my rucksack cutting my shoulders and looking for Interstate 80. I wanted to believe what they believed, but could not. Something drove me on. Kept me searching, questioning. I should have just thrown the whole thing up and gotten a job and a wife and a mortgage right then.

I took a drink. I watched Harry. He looked strong in the firelight. You couldn't see the blemishes. There was passion in his eyes. He was a broken, old drunk. I knew it. I suppose he did too, but he wouldn't admit it to himself. So maybe he wasn't really broken, not yet —that would take another day or so. Defiance flashed in his grin, defiance beyond bravado, something more than the courage of the bottle. The bottle had stopped working for him a long time before. But there was something somewhere that kept him going, that kept him going on beyond lost hope, some unrealized idea of redemption that was just beyond the next horizon, or maybe at the bottom of the next bottle. In his grin, maybe forced, maybe real, I don't know, but I knew I was seeing the road firsthand. I saw a man who had gone his own way. (No choice of his own, it had been the bottle and this unquenchable thirst that had put him and kept him on this road.) His road wasn't a romantic dream, it was Kerouac's *Road,* the road that Kerouac called a "nightmare" in the paragraph that we skip when we're young. (Go back and read it for yourself.)

This road is the horror of the outcast. Harry the outcast, the cast away, excluded by a society where he did not belong, a mariner marooned on islands surrounded by seas of civilization, yet more distant than any Pacific atoll. But, "Good God," they were indeed pacific islands--islands of refuge, Skid Rows. Pacific, peaceful in their way, where a man could drink and piss and pass out on the street and nobody gave a damn. Just what Harry required—to be let alone. Not deserted, but solitary all the same, wreckage-strewn beaches where no one would question why you were chugging 32oz of mouthwash at eight on a Sunday morning or taking shots from bottles of lemon extract on a Tuesday afternoon. You might wake up minus your shoes, less your empty wallet if you still had one. Maybe even steal your pants if you hadn't pissed them too bad. "We took care of each other," Harry told me. "See a man sleeping on the Row, we leave him alone. We see a man shaking, see a man curled up like he's in his momma's belly, we know he's got them DTs. We give him a nip. Nip of nectar, keep them DT's away for another day. Nothing worse than running out."

In my ignorance those lost islands were romance to me, as they had been to Jack. Harry had known them all—the Bowery in lower Manhattan, Sand Street across the river, the Nickel in LA, Vine in Philly, Frisco's Embarcadero. Columbus Street, home to City Lights Books, off which, Jack sat back to wall in an alley to be alone with his port. All Romance. Dover in Boston, "Irish always help a man down on his luck," but Dover was death in the winter. "Saw a man froze solid. Even his pint froze solid, had to thaw it under m' coat." He knew Memphis' Clark, Congress in Houston. And up north, Michigan Avenue. He had the *Madison Blues* in Chi Town and the *Kansas City Blues* on Main.

"Years ago, knew a man in Laramie, carried 'round a wrench. Tapped into automobile radiators. Back in the old days you could drink that shit. 100 proof. Bit of a bite, but stopped the demon. Didn't use no cup. Sonofabitch laying on his back in the street with his mouth wide open draining them chrome Satans. Get you drunk too. Not good drunk. Drunk to keep off the shakes till ya get some real stuff in ya. Course, they changed that shit. Antifreeze'll kill ya nowadays. Changed that sonofabitch. Man tapping a shiny Cadillac. Joking that Caddy's top-shelf. Better 'an a Pink Lady. Just like gin he says, laying on his back and grinning and draining that sucker. And here's the joke. Caddy had that new-fangled antifreeze. That green shit. He drank it down and whoops … whoops … he's all doubled up. Staggering. Groping for a wall. Going blind. Blinded. Rolling on the ground. Puking hisself. Shitting hisself. Convulsing. Killed him dead.

"Saw it with my own eyes."

And we laughed. Harry and I laughed. God help me, and God help this poor man's soul, but it was all a lark. Harry was laughing when he told me, and I was laughing along. Rifling a dead man's pockets to find his pint. And the punchline was that it was as frozen as he was. Harry had to thaw it out under his coat, cold as hell. Man drains a car's radiator, the joke's on him. They changed the formula.

"Them things oughta carry warning labels." And we laughed.

As we sat and laughed on that placid lake the old Skid Rows were being washed away—old Rowers, no place to go. Flops and fleabags, cheap hotels and SRO's, nickel-a-night dormitories, all going away.

Nobody wants to see bums anymore. "Don't know why? Not hurting nobody. They got them parks and planters. Pee-destrian malls." He spit the words out with distaste. "Hell, I been in those shelters. Shelters ain't no missions. Missions give a man hope. Hallelujah boys run them missions, good hearts. Listen and sing and give 'em a smile. And they give ya a square meal. Man knows the taste of liquor, knows the way we is. Got his self free, come back to help. Shelters, social workers, Cadillac preachers, don't know nothing 'bout drinking. Nowadays shelters full of crazy people talking to themselves, swing at the air with quick, closed fists. Shelters full of rules. Shelters make you stand in line half the night. Got them schedules. Schedule this and schedule that.

"What the hell 'm supposed to do? Hell, I got my own schedule. Come and go. Go and Come. Get my load on and go to sleep. Get up when I want. Get out when I want. Not standing in the cold all day. I got your nickel, gimme a bed. Rest my head. Ain't no beds no more. What'd I do? I ain't no hobo. Ain't no 'bo. Hobo. Oh, no. Give me a quiet room. Sleep ta noon."

For all his talk of the road, Harry wasn't really a traveler. The road was a mistake that he'd get himself into between bars, a prepaid trip out of town on the Hound when local authorities had had their fill of him. Or he'd attach himself to someone, somehow going to Denver or New Orleans or the Dakota Badlands—and at the time it seems like a good idea till you wake behind some cowboy bar with piss-stained pants and puke on your shirt and wonder —"How the hell? How the hell? What the hell happened?" Given a steady supply of booze, and maybe a warm place to rest, and maybe some food on occasion, Harry'd stay in one spot forever. But when you're Harry, people get sick of you and move you along. And sometimes when you're drunk, in a blackout, moving seems like a good idea. But eventually you get to a point where places don't matter anymore. One's as good as another. Something else is what matters.

Harry took the bottle up and looked through it into the firelight. There wasn't much left. He lifted it to his lips and swallowed it down. I don't think he even tasted it. He was like a dog with a chunk of meat—it just goes down. He pushed himself up and walked over to the lake and flung the bottle into the water. "Bombs away."

He stood for a while, came back and sat at the fire. "You hungry?"

"Naw. Maybe. I don't know. Stew is cooked to shit."

He was right. It was sludge in the bottom of the pot. I added water from the lake and gave it a stir. I didn't care. I wasn't hungry, and not a little drunk. I wasn't used to straight whiskey on an empty stomach. "I'll fix us up some," said more from form than desire. I went into the cabin to get bowls and spoons and such. There was a ladle on the wall. I grabbed it. Too bad we didn't have some rolls and butter. I looked in the cupboard for crackers, and as I opened the door remembered the gin. I feared as I reached for it that Harry had gotten into it. But he hadn't.

A surprise. Harry smiled. "There ya go, son. Regular cornucopia we got us.

"People pay good money for this," he said. "I'm thinking maybe we can start something. Got good service," he motioned with his head toward me. "Couple of days to clean out the system. Dry out. Out in the country. Take time from the boozing." It seemed like a good idea. Maybe I could help Harry, help get him cleaned up. We talked about who might own the land and how they wouldn't be adverse to us setting up a drunk farm—that's what Harry called it. A refuge where a sporting man could clean himself up and get off the sauce. We could make wine, maybe some apple jack in the fall. I was too drunk to question why a place that catered to cleaning up drunks would be making booze. I didn't know at the time, but sobering up was Harry's idea toward the end of every bottle. Maybe it's every drunk's idea when he's on the lee shore of a load. It's easy to quit when you've got a belly full and a nip left. But you know that you aren't going to stop drinking any more than you're going to start a drunk farm or build a boat and sail it around the world—someday.

About halfway through the gin I got the bowls and spoons and such. Harry took a bite of the mulligan and looked at me. "Not too bad." I took some too.

"What are these black things?" I asked, more to myself than to Harry, but he answered.

"Peas. Peas, yes indeed, I believe them's peas."

They were the right size. They were round. Whatever. The mulligan was salty and peppery. The texture was odd. The meat chunks? The vegetables? Maybe potatoes?  All had the same muted color and mushy consistency. And the black peas for punctuation. But not rotten. I was drunk and hungry when the food hit me.

"Time for a little after-dinner indulgence," Harry said and stood up. "I think I'll just get that bottle of crème de menthe we've been saving. We'll have us a toast." He never stopped. And this after he had just told me that he was going to stop drinking and clean himself up.

"Lord looks after drunks.'" He passed the sharp-edged bottle to me, and I took a swig of the green liqueur.

The crème de menthe was a mistake. The stew was a mistake. And the gin and most of the whiskey. It all happened quickly. The world was spinning. I stood to move. Puked in the sand where I sat. Couldn't stand, couldn't sit, rolled down on my side and into the puke. Vomited again and rolled back and it was on my arm. It shocked me, first time I had ever puked on myself. I made it over to the treeline, up and staggering, the world heaving under me, on my knees, leaned heavily against a pine and puked and puked and puked until there was nothing left, and my stomach still convulsed. I looked up. A pair of eyes shone in the shadows. Quite drunk, I could only move from tree to tree. It took my all to reach the fire and sit down hard. Harry held up the bottle for me to take a drink. He was a madman. I shook my head. Some hound on the edge of the light was sniffing what I had just puked.

More dogs were moving in the brush.

"Ain't all it's cracked up to be," Harry laughed a bitter laugh.

"What?"

"Sporting man. Ain't all it's cracked up to be. Ain't that at all."

I'd had enough and staggered off to bed.

# the faith of the fisherman

Getting a load on, that's the romance of the road.
Right?

But I'd gotten carried away. Here I was back to Paradise, feeling like Hell. On the bunk across, he was on his back with his head twisted to the side, his mouth thrown open, a streak of spittle threatening to drop. Stubble marked his cheeks and chin. His hair stood stiff and crazy. I turned away and lay with my face to the wall until the need to pee drove me out of my bunk. My head pounded when I moved. I peed in the trees and then went to the edge of the lake and kneeled on the sand and splashed my face with the cold water. I took the risk of drinking some from cupped hands. The sun was well up. I'd promised myself to be up at dawn to watch the rising sun. I hadn't wound my watch. Mid-morning I guessed. I ran my hand across my face and felt my stubble.

The firepit was a shambles. The big pot was turned over and off to the side. Brown and olive-green bits of cardboard were scatted about. The ground was torn up. The dogs. They'd gotten into the stew and the rations after we'd gone to bed. Well, I hoped they puked their brains our like I had. I made hot water for coffee.

I sipped the coffee and hazarded a smoke, finished the butt and lit another, head-sore and soul-miserable. I needed more water. Cautious after getting sick on the stew, I remembered the iodine tablets from the rations and tried a few in my canteen. Better than nothing.

I noticed the quiet only when a jet flew far overhead and disturbed it, no bird or car or even rustle from wind. A fish broke the surface of the lake. Silent, concentric ripples spread and faded. I felt the stillness draw me in. I thought of E.B. White's groin of death.

I rose and shook it off and resolved to action. Those damn rations had made me sick. I'd catch some fish. I'd read Hemingway. I knew how easy it was to fish. Love-sore-adolescent in the North Woods, war-wrecked-vet on the *Big Two-Hearted River*, rich-old-sot in the Gulf Stream, catching fish was never the problem with Hemingway. Looking into the lake I could see the fish. There they were, swimming slowly through the lily pads in the shallows off to the side of the ruined pier. I could see insects on the water and rings where fish rose and insects vanished. And I could see swirls where fins moved under the surface, even an occasional splash in the middle of the lake. As if on cue, a huge bird crashed down and snatched some poor sonofafish to its eternal reward. So I knew the fish were there. How hard could it be? It all seemed obvious enough. Rods and reels and hooks and bobbers, simply put them together and add a worm. Cast a line out. And I would be fishing, waiting for dinner, surviving off the land. Maybe the wine would turn out to be white?

It didn't take long to find what I needed in the boathouse. After all this *was* a sportsman's camp. In a few minutes I had my fishing line in the lake and was looking forward to nice meal. I stood on the shore. My bobber floated softly, unmoved. I don't know exactly what I was expecting. A fish to latch on and the bobber to, well, bob? That's what it was, wasn't it? A bobber? I waited. I set the rod down and got a log from next to the firepit, watching carefully the bobber. I pulled the log close and sat on it and waited, my attention focused razor-sharp on the small red and white float. Smoked another cigarette, the bobber bobbed. A fish! I watched it bob, then stop. Now what? I reeled it in. The worm was gone. Perhaps I hadn't read Hemingway quite closely enough.

I put on another worm. Cast it out. 'Set the hook,' the phrase popped into my mind. Of course, I had to set the hook. When the fish bit I had to yank the line and set the hook. Good old Hemingway, that was the trick. The bobber, after a time, bobbed and I yanked to set the hook and the bobber flew into the air and up with the sinker and now naked hook. Too hard, I'd have to be more careful. I waited and watched. The fish, the lake, they weren't playing into my narrative. I don't know how long I waited. Not too long. I wanted to catch fish. I got up and peered into water stained like strong tea. A fish swirled away. It was small, too small. Not big enough for a meal, too small for the hook. A minnow, just nibbling. I wanted a big one like I had seen the bird take.

I was figuring it out. What I needed to do was to go where the fish were.

Dragging the Grumman from the boathouse, banging paddles and rod, clumping my sneakers on the aluminum hull, was more than enough to scare all the fish from the weeds at our end of the lake. I paddled as quietly as I could toward deeper water. I slid the bobber up the line so the hook and bait sunk deep. Dropped my line. Waited.

Here I was on the lake, still, peaceful, timeless. A bird, not the one I had seen before, this one much smaller, a lovely color blue, swooped from the trees and plunged into the water and came up with a flash of silver in its beak. That was timeless too, sustenance for the bird. But the silver minnow snatched from life in an unexpected instant, not so peaceful for the minnow. I sat as still as I could. I watched a turtle climb up on a log near the shore. A snake, long as an arm, swam along, head just breaching the surface. Here I was catching my own dinner. My rustic, vagabond buddy awaiting my bountiful return. I tried to forget about the minnows and birds and their life and death struggles. I was safe and trying to be still. But nothing was hitting the hook. My bobber wasn't bobbing.

I could dream and idyll and enjoy my fishing so long as I had faith—faith in the fish and their hunger and their ability to find my worm in the great expanse of sameness that was the lake. But I began to doubt. I could only see a foot or two through the stained water. How far could the fish see? What were the odds that one would swim close enough to find my bait? I had no concept of their world. I could only imagine what I knew, what I could perceive, and what I would think if I were swimming around under the surface. The more I thought about it, the less faith I had—I wanted certainty. I wanted immediate proof—but the fish weren't biting. Who knew? Real fishermen had faith, faith in the habits of the fish and their hunger and would wait for hours for the fish that certainly would strike. But not me, not that day.

I couldn't wait. I kept reeling in and casting out for a better spot, looking off toward the far end of the lake, wondering if I should find a fresh worm or use something else all altogether. There were lures in the tackle box. I didn't have any experience with them, but I knew enough that you cast them out and reel them back in. I should have brought the box. That's why you had a box, so you could take it with you in the boat. Alright. I'd go back to get the tackle box and more worms. I'd be damned. I was going to catch a fish.

Harry was awake and out and standing on the shore waiting for me. "Land ho," he called out with a smile, very friendly.

"Three sheets to the wind," I thought.

"Wondered where ya got too. Heard some banging. That you? Saw ya out there. Must be biting good? What'd ya catch?"

"Tackle box," I said. "And more worms." My tone, abrupt, made the old man frown and look down. I felt apologetic, but not enough to apologize. A lost-looking, long-eared hound wearing a collar watched from the edge of the woods. Was it the one who had been sniffing my vomit? I didn't want to think about it. I went in the boathouse, grabbed the tackle box, and on a whim decided to grab a spare rod—there was a mess of them in a corner. I picked a nice little number with a spinning reel. Mixed in was a long-handled net. I grabbed that. Hiding behind it, an ugly-looking spear —a trident—three rusty prongs on a pole. I grabbed that too.

"Good luck," the old man called out. He was trying to be friendly. I kicked my sneakers off to keep from thumping the bottom of the boat. Stealth was the plan. I was serious. Quiet and slow I paddled. I stalked my game. I was getting the hang of this fishing stuff. I was headed to the far shore. A gentle point of land pushed out into the water to hide the north end of the lake. The shore was higher on this point, the trees immense. Unlike the dense scrub that shielded the rest of the lakeshore, the ground under these trees was clear, the underbrush choked by suffocating needles. Tall, majestic trunks, branchless columns rising to dense, dark green domes impressed me with their solemnity, a cathedral rising above the smaller trees that surrounded us and the lakeshore.

When I rounded the point I could see that there was a lot more lake than I had thought. It was a long paddle. I stopped in the middle and drifted. It was so lonely. To cast and reel or bait a hook on a bobber seemed hopeless. Who knew what was down there? I had at least seen fish in the shallows. I paddled on. At the far, north end of the lake there were dead, bone-bleached tree trunks standing in the water. Ten, fifteen, maybe twenty feet tall, they were scattered and mostly branchless—cylindrical tombstones in a watery graveyard. I paddled between them. There was something defiant about them, as if they had refused death, stood strong against the Reaper. Others had surrendered and were now broken off, trunks fallen in the water. But for those who had surrendered and fallen, their stumps were reborn to become tiny, fecund islands. Rising above the water, inches just in diameter, moss and small bushes and even little trees grew on these stumps. Worlds all unto themselves. Magical little places. A snag, a fallen tree, caught the side of my canoe and lifted it and almost upset me. I had to be slow and careful. The water was clogged with skinny shoots of grass. There was movement off to my right and ripples on the surface. This was fish country! I saw a fish dart away. I had visual proof. It was shallow here, too shallow to paddle, so I pushed in and glided as far as the grass would allow. I waited and watched and held as still as I could for as long as I could stand it. Gradually the shadows of fish emerged, and I could see the little swirls on the top of the water when they moved.

I got the spinning reel and rod, banging the side of Grumman, clumsy. A half-dozen swirls in the water responded. If I'd been more careful ... but there *were* fish. I picked a lure that looked like a minnow. It was jointed in the middle and had two treble hooks, one on its belly and another replacing its tail. It was a mean-looking device and fit my mood. I gave it good cast, let it sink a moment, reeled it in. I snagged, gave a sharp tug and was free. I cast over and over again. I was fishing.

Over and over casting. Catching a little snag now and then. Maybe fish were hitting on the lure. I didn't know, didn't catch any. I was trying to feel if a fish hit the lure, trying to drop my cast into a clear spot. The bottom was dead leaves that I pulled up with the lure and filled the air with the miasma of decay. I felt my pocket for a smoke, but had left them in the cabin. The old man was probably smoking them. I was just casting and reeling mechanically. It seemed futile. The tackle box had a dozen or more lures. There was a red and white one, like the working-end of a spoon, with a treble hook. Another had a little chrome propeller and a heavy flat triangle of lead and more of the ubiquitous treble hooks. A third looked like a tiny banana with a flattened end, this with three treble hooks, all abstractions. I preferred the ones that looked like little fish, wood and well-crafted, with tiny keels to keep them down. I tried different ones, picked a guy that looked home-made and tied it on. No hits, but a snag I couldn't free. I gave a hard tug and the line snapped. I felt bad losing the lure, something important about it. Someone had made it and used it, caught fish with it. And I had lost it.

I would get it back. I tried to paddle, then push with the paddle to where it was snagged, but it was too weedy. There's no simple way to exit a canoe. I couldn't just stand and step out, but I could sit on the seat and swing my legs outboard and kind of hop off. I dipped a rail and almost turned it over, leaned back to balance, my hand on the seat, the canoe slipped away, and I fell in. It was all shockingly quick and awkward. I was sitting in the shallow water, wet from my chest down. I instinctively looked up to see who had seen me. No one of course. Well, it wasn't winter, and I wasn't going to freeze. And I hadn't dumped the boat and lost the tackle box. I waded over to where the lure had disappeared and felt around till I found the string and followed it to the lure. Then something big, moving quickly, attracted my attention. It wasn't just a dart and swirl like I had seen before. I could actually trace where this fish was going. It was swimming strongly. I could see a flash of a fin in the shallows. Was it running away or chasing something? I could see its back and dorsal fin. It was big, a couple of feet maybe. I thought of dinner. I thought of my bare toes!

I forgot the lost lure, didn't even consider the rod and reel and treble hooks. I'd net it. I could follow the creature's path and note where it rested. I'd just scoop it up. I was calm and shuffled my feet so as not to splash—the good hunter. Stealth. I raised the net and the fish bolted. "Stupid." I could see the shadow of the net on the water, so could the fish. Hunters always crept up to animals downwind. I had to be down-sun. There would be no shadows. Shuffling in a circle, slowly I crept. I could see it in the shallows. I held the net high, then smashed it down over the beast. A flash of fin and it was in, then out and away. I watched it move off, then slow and stop in the weeds. I'd almost had it. I just had to hold the net flat against the bottom till I knew it was trapped. I'd circle around again. But this time, halfway through my circle the fish dashed toward me. I swung with the net and chased it back. I stirred up mud and leaves across the bottom. I lost it. Then ripples a few yards off headed toward the shore. But rather than a definite shore like the south end of the lake, the water carried on into the living trees, into a swamp with hummocks holding two or three trees and interspersed with pools of dark water. I could hardly walk with all the tangle. Little room to swing the net, but I could follow and track the fish until ... the spear ... of course. I'd spear it.

I liked this better. No stalking. I splashed with my feet to scare my prey deeper into the swamp, the ratio of water to land decreasing with each step. I figured it would get shallower and narrower, which it did. I don't' know what the fish thought. It really didn't try to get past me. I'd read that salmon spawn in the same streams that they were born in. This fish wasn't a salmon, but perhaps this fish was headed home? Maybe there was another lake ahead that it knew as a sanctuary? It paused for a moment. I let fly the spear. A miss. The fish went into the next dark pool. A throw and another miss. It was hard aiming the spear. I threw again and the fish moved into a shallow that was cut off by a fallen trunk, a dead end. I had it. No spear throws now. I charged with jabs and thrusts as the fish thrashed frantically in shallow water. Splashes of fish and feet and the tail up and my spear in. Thrust, thrust in panic. Fish, still flipping frantically on mossy-land mud and sand and shallow, dark water, desperate to avoid my trident.

I felt its struggle but I could not stop.

At last, I put a spike into its flank. I had it on the end of my spear and held it high and then put it on the bank—still thrashing. How could I stop it? I put my foot on the head and pulled out the spear, then thrust again and again and again and with each thrust the fish thrashed less.

It was a miracle that I didn't stab my foot. I put the carcass in the bottom of the canoe and paddled back. I was determined to eat it. Kill to kill—that would have been too much for me. The old man was taken aback by the sight of the fish. It looked pretty bad.

"Youse all wet," he said

I said nothing.

I dug back into my Hemingway memory. How did he cook a fish? I slit it down the belly as best I could and pulled out the entrails and tossed them into the lake. A swarm of little guys attacked them. I cut off the head and tail. There was cast iron pan in the cabin. I stoked the fire and put the pan on. Had Hemingway used oil or butter or lard or bacon grease? Didn't matter, I didn't have any. Did Kerouac ever fish? I couldn't remember. No, he made sandwiches and rode the bus. I put the fish in the hot pan and flipped it with a spatula. I didn't know when it was done, cooked too long and hot and burned and stuck to the pan. I got some forks and plates and shoved broken bits onto the plates. I wanted to act like it was all ok. I wanted to keep my front up for the old man—like pulp-of-fish-flesh was what I had intended all along and char-of-fish-skin was my fine cooking. The old man was polite. He took a tentative bite, chewed a tad and carefully pulled tiny bones from his mouth. I did the same.

Harry thanked me for a "wonderful lunch" and decided on a nap. Drink and sleep seemed to be all he did. Stupid old sot.

I haven't been fishing since.

# an allegory

All the fish in my lake added to the fish in every lake and added again to all the fish in the all the oceans would not equal the cycles of birth and rebirth endured by bodhisattva Avalokiteśvara. Not numberless cycles, but numbered—each cycle, whether woman or man, rich, poor, virile, crippled by beauty or by the face-eating horror of leprosy—each remembered in suffering. Rebirths as dogs and camels, as fishes and fishers, exquisite butterfly or offal-eating beetle.

Each remembered as Avalokiteśvara turns to the final cycle of release, to the Nirvana sought for aeons. Attention now turns to a wailing from the world below, voices upturned, thrashing in their own cycles of life and death and suffering. Down looks the great bodhisattva, who on the precipice of release hears the cries of pain and will leave us not, will forgo release. Like the Christ, this bodhisattva will take on the suffering of the world so that we might be released from our own cycles of birth and rebirth. Avalokiteśvara shall suffer, so that we shall not.

Avalokiteśvara, this bodhisattva of compassion, was Jack's bodhisattva, touchstone of Jack's own search for deliverance from the demons that put him on his road. For all the hedonism, carefully read, Jack's novels are pilgrimages toward spiritual fulfillment. Jack's thinly-veiled fictions are seekers of Neal's antecedentless *It,* trapped tragically in the sensual. And just as Jack was my window into the jazz and the booze, he was equally my window into a path of deliverance from my own demons.

While the old man slept I walked a sandy track through the brush and wound my way through the tangle of pine to the point with the cathedral of trees, drawn to it as sanctuary. No one had seen me, but I knew I had experienced something terrible, and I now sought refuge. In *Dharma Bums,* Jack writes how he sought refuge in meditation. I would do the same. I would seek refuge in this Dharma.

My grove was soft and dark. I sat cross-legged on a carpet of brown needles, back against brown wood. Trunks clear of branches for twenty feet above my head, then closed-tight with the ever green to offer a comforting shield from the sky. I would meditate. That was my answer. But like Hemingway's fishing, I really had no idea. Palms up-stretched, breath mitigated, eyes closed, I tried to still my mind, to empty it of my distress. I didn't know how. I kept thinking of the fish thrashing. Had I waited with the bobber and hook I would have caught some fish. I would have killed them and cooked them. The outcome would have been the same for the fish. Would it have been ok? Would *I* have been ok? I had eaten fish a thousand times. All killed by someone. Why couldn't I have just waited? Fished with the hook and line. The three-pronged spear, I shuddered when I thought of it. It wasn't just the killing. It was my frenzy. The fish had tried its best to flee. Why not let it alone? It wasn't like pulling some anonymous creature up on a hook. No, while it tried to escape, and while I pursued, a bond—

hunter and hunted—had been formed. I had killed some part of me. I had felt the lust of blood that I could not stop, that frenzy of killing was in me. I was thinking, thinking too fast. I wasn't supposed to think, wanted to stop thinking, turn away. Kerouac, how did he meditate? Avalokiteśvara, where was *my* bodhisattva? Hemingway and his fishing and his one true sentence, he didn't have any qualms killing fish. The fish in the too-shallow, dark-pool swamp, tail thrashing. I had an essay due the day after spring break on Faulkner—Faulkner and his damn *Bear*, the old man with the shabby .22 under the tree and the trapped squirrels. The killing so easy and perfect in the books. The fish gone forever. Avalokiteśvara looking down from a place that was not the sky. I couldn't stop. I couldn't sit. Meditation wasn't my way. The Dharma, the spiritual, it hadn't worked for Kerouac, not in the end. Just a story for fools. I got up and walked back off the point and followed the sandy track away from camp. Motion—that was my path—motion and adventure and myself.

The sandy track wound this way and that, generally alongside the lake. The brush thinned in places and closed in others. I needed to keep moving. I got hold of myself. I'd do a little exploring, maybe make a circle of the lake. The track led to a swampy area of dark pools. I turned away and went up a rise to a bright, open wood. It was like stepping into a park, spacious and inviting and gratifying. This was the rustic idyll I had imagined. All it lacked were benches and a gazebo. The trees were widely spaced, smaller than those on the point, a different species. I could walk undisturbed, free of any path. The sun shown through gaily in islands of joy. I wandered north to miss the swamp. There was a low carpet of brush, new green-spring leaves, ankle high, easy to walk through, a few low plants budding and a flat, dry moss in patches of sandy soil. Tangles of thorn-covered vine hung between some of the trees, but the overall effect was inviting, and I easily skirted their obstruction. A scraggly bush, spots of color, spring flowers, bright yellow that didn't fit the pattern of green and brown, drew my attention. It was a welcome contrast to the muted swamp behind me. I walked over and almost stumbled into a pit. There was a depression, half-walled with brick. More bricks were scatted about when I looked for them. I could make out the remnants of a hearth and its chimney fallen to the side, bricks marking an outline like a fallen tree. The faded track of a sandy road ran through a canyon of trees, two lines of trees, parallel, and running off into the woods—their spacing just wide enough for what? A wagon? Ancient, but not yet overgrown, I supposed the shade of the established trees kept the center of the track free from fresh growth. Someone lined the ancient ones up long ago. A bit of backwoods landscaping? The track went off away from the lake. It was tempting, but I thought I should stick to my circuit of the water. I'd need to head east in a bit. I didn't want to get stuck walking back in the dark. I poked around the ruins. An old cellar of some sort? I could make out the lines of what was a house. Odd that someone should live way out here. The sun was slanting through the trees. It was all quite lovely. A low foundation of cement standing alone off to the right caught my attention. It was just a foundation half-wrecked in the woods. But I walked over and around it and touched it. It was a story of failure, abandonment in an ancient tongue that I could not read. I could see another road led to it. It was overgrown, long untraveled.

The park went as far as my vision, well-spaced trees gradually overlapping in the distance to form a wall of trunks, but with no sense of confinement. Where I wandered all was spacious. I walked from this thing to the next, a stand of feral daffodils that I approached or a soggy depression that turned me aside. The ground of sand and moss gave way to low brush. Ahead, some trunks of the trees were blackened. There'd been a fire. I crossed a trench only few feet wide that looked fresh—a few years perhaps, as opposed to the many decades, or maybe century, that marked the wrecked house. I was surprised that so insignificant of a trench could halt the burning. Beyond the trench, small trees were brown and dead. The lower branches of the taller trees were also brown, but up top they carried green needles. The underbrush, much denser than in the park, was charred and black, but with hints of green shoots and buds poking through—life springing from apparent death. There was an abundance of the thorn-covered vine, black and brittle, cooked by the fire, and I could snap it easily to make my way. In the burnt-over wood the straight trunks of the parkland gave way to crooked, misshapen stalks with twists and turns and multiple trunks. It was a history of many fires long past, trees burnt and reborn in new directions. Green shoots from the black trunks went off in crazy angles. Though burnt, I could see the underbrush had been thick here. This section of wood had burnt time and time again. The denser underbrush carried the flames. These trees had suffered many times. Like the wrecked foundation, the scorched woods held a perverse fascination, as if the natural state of the woods were not enough for me. I craved more, craved the novelty of feral flowers and brick foundations and past drama in traces of fire and failure.

One tree caught my eye. It was burnt and broken, maybe hit by lightning years ago, maybe the fatal lightning that had started the fire. It looked like Edvard Munch's painting *The Scream*. It made me laugh aloud. My madness with the fish—I had read too much into it, as if it were literature, not reality. It was nothing. It was just a fish. That's what you get from reading Faulkner all winter, every damn thing a symbol of something else and that something else is something else again. It didn't really mean a thing. The old house and the ditch made me feel I wasn't alone in the woods. There was still civilization and not simply the primal struggling of the dying fish. Off to the left I saw two deer—one, full-grown, a few dozen yards away, and another, a tiny thing with huge eyes, watched motionless not more than ten feet from me. I could have almost stepped on it. The big one flashed its tail and crashed across before me while the fawn watched with its great eyes. I didn't want to scare it, so I turned away from the fire crew's trench and moved off. I was in another landscape. It was glorious with the setting sun to my back. The amber light cut through in shafts. Spring ferns gaining their foothold in the sandy soil were brushed aside. I picked up a closed pinecone and put it in my pocket as a souvenir.

A tire—a rubber, automobile tire lay on the earth with a tree growing through it. How long had it been here? Who had left it? Who had fixed their flat here in the pines? How many years ago? I could just put my two hands around the trunk. How long for a six-inch diameter pine to grow? Some thorns stood in my way, and I had to walk around them. I expected to come upon the lake and its dead, bone-like tree trunks in a minute or two. It seemed so obvious. Where was it? I began to doubt my direction. Should I stop? No. Go on. Quicken my step. It was a subtle shift, another kind of watershed moment, when curiosity became compulsion. I went on. I could see clear sky above the lake. The bucolic image of the deer and the idyllic park of trees was still with me. I turned to where, ahead, the tops of the trees stopped, relieved to have found the lake at last. I just had to keep close and follow the shoreline around to get back to the camp. I wasn't yet concerned. I moved into low ground, a good sign for finding the lake. The underbrush was thick, plants with tangled stalks. I had to skirt them and found patches of the thorny vine. I moved in a crooked path, but keeping the clear sky above the lake as my goal. I doubted for a second. I might have found the wrong lake, but shook off my fears. No, I was on the right path I assured myself as I tore at a cruel vine that blocked my progress.

Okay. So, I didn't have a lot of experience with nature. But I wasn't totally stupid. I knew that the sun rose in the east and set in the west. I knew that the sun had come up over the lake, and it would set behind the cabin at the south end of the lake. I had started out in late afternoon—maybe that wasn't such a good idea. But I figured to go around the lake. If I kept the afternoon sun on my left I'd be going north, then with the sun at my back to head east, then the sun on my right and south and down the far side of the lake. When the lakeshore turned to the right I'd be at the bottom of the lake, and I could come up and around and be back at the camp—setting sun in my face. Easy. But in the spring, in the fall, any season I guess, the sun is actually a bit south. The angles aren't quite square, west to north, east to south, not quite 90 degrees. And, I guess, in truth, I wasn't really paying attention. I had a native, good sense of direction and simply followed it. I'd turned away from the swamp. I should have crossed it to continue my circumnavigation of the lake, should have stayed close to the shore. Then I was distracted by the ruins and wandering across the pathless, park-like flat. I followed the fire crew's trench and each little obstruction of brush and thorn, and the fawn too, had shifted me in an only vaguely realized change of course. A step to the left, turn and two steps to the right, the crossing over to avoid the dense underbrush, all combined until I was lost, but didn't know it yet. The lake, it was just ahead I assured myself, creating my own reality, everything was fine. I was right on track. Just keep moving ahead. Go on. (Take another drink.) I abandoned the idea of circumnavigating the lake. I turned directly toward the clear sky where the trees stopped. It was getting late. I'd find the damn thing and head right back on the near shore—walking in the water if I had to. The vines with the thorns were tangling me up. It was harder now to find a route between the patches. The vines were too supple to snap cleanly. Their sinews simply folded when I tried to break them. I had no choice but to move them aside and climb through, horrible things, thick as a pencil, with tack-sharp thorns like a rosebush. They grew more tangled. I tried to hurry, snagged my cheek, pulled it way and ripped the flesh, blood on the back of my hand when I wiped across it, missed my eye by an inch. A wall of pain between me and the lake. A wall all the worse because I could see into and through it, could see my goal of clear sky. I could only pick my way, moving the vines as I pushed carefully through them. I tore at one, and in the attack, pulled others down on myself. They went from ground to treetop. It was slow going. I wondered, only half in jest, if they were a kind of carnivorous plant that would trap and prick me a thousand times and nourish on my essence, evil roots drinking my blood as it dripped into the soil. Still, I was making progress. Slowly. I tried to be careful. I didn't want to leave an eyeball hanging on a vine. The sunlight was all but gone, just touching the tops of the trees, descending so quickly. My impatience, I pushed hard through the last few feet and tore my shirt and ripped an arm with scratches. It was painful, stupid, foolish, panicked. I broke through in a final push of dense underbrush.

It wasn't the lake at all. The normal-size trees did indeed stop, but not for lake. Instead, I was faced with a field of stunted pines, tangled and overgrown, some blackened with fire, impenetrable, ugly, unworldly. I'd stepped into nature's joke. A miniature forest, but a nasty, little forest that I couldn't wade through. And even if I did? To what end? I had never seen anything like it. I stood on tiptoe to look over the tops of the trees, if I could call them that. But they *were* trees, not the tangled vines, trees low and densely packed and off to the horizon. There was nothing for it but to go back through the tangle of vines and try to pick up the road or the trench to follow. I had to control myself now. I was as careful as I could stand to be. I had a spare shirt in my pack. The one I was wearing was a wreck. But where was the cabin and shirt and rucksack and Harry?

Whatever path I had taken through the thorn was lost. I tried to angle away toward the south. I found the firebreak and the burnt wood and *The Scream*. But no flowers or abandoned house. I went back to the *The Scream*. Was it the one I had seen? I should have marked it. Where was the tire with the tree? It should be around here. I was walking fast. There, the tire. No? This was a faded whitewall. Was the other? I couldn't remember. I should have noticed. I was in trouble now. The sun was down. I was getting scared. If I could find the swamp I could find the lake, but where was the swamp? I couldn't keep the sun on my left now. Would I hit the road? I wouldn't know which way to go. Should I just walk on? I didn't want to leave my stuff. Didn't want to leave the old man. My shirt was ripped. Who would pick up a boy with a ripped shirt in the middle of nothing in the night? If I left, what would the old drunk do? We were a team. I didn't want to be alone. No, I wanted to find the cabin.

Everything was different in the dark. I found the drop and the hill to the swamp and looked down. I wasn't going in there—jumping from hummock to hummock in the dark. And it was really black down there in the shadows. And the snake I saw in the lake?

I tried to follow the edge. Was it the same hill and swamp? Was this the park-like wood from before? It seemed denser, harder to get through. The malevolent vines filled in the gaps where the dead branches of the trees didn't reach. I tried to go slowly. I was racing against my growing panic. The tree growing inside the tire. There it was, or was it another one? I put my hands around the trunk. It was smaller than before, much smaller. How many tires with trees growing through them could there be? I knew I was supposed to stop when I got lost in the woods. Why couldn't I stop when it became apparent that stopping was the solution? Wasn't I willing to admit that I was lost, disoriented, defeated? I tried to reason it out. I told myself that I wasn't in danger. I just had to be reasonable. I wasn't far from people. There were old roads all over the place. I could sit and wait till daylight. It wasn't cold. I wasn't going to freeze. I wasn't in the desert dying of thirst. I had food in my stomach. I could wait-out the night easy. I could follow the dawn. I'd hit a road or something. I could follow it. Make some markers so I knew where I had been. Who cared about the cabin? Stupid sot could fend for himself. He could have my stuff. In the morning I could find the road where the stupid truck had dumped us off. Backtrack. Get my stuff. I hated to lose my journal. "It's okay," I kept telling myself as I crashed and scratched and stumbled and blindly pushed through the tangles.

Look at the underside of a pine sometime. It's a pincushion of dead, thin branches. Try that in the dark. Minutes, ten minutes, fifteen? I looked back at the path I had cleared for myself. It was hopeless. I'd only gone a few yards. I needed a machete. I wanted to turn back, but to what? I wanted to cry, but to whom? Something wouldn't let me stop and wait or turn aside or go back or give up, although all my logic said I must. It got darker. I went into a section of reddish-dark, spindly trees with peeling bark. The ground was clear, no thorn vines, no low, dry branches. But as I walked through the spindly trees closed in. Soon they were so closely spaced I had to turn to pass. Then I was in another open section. I walked for some time and realized there wasn't any pattern. The woods on all sides was open and dark. What had been the freedom of widely-spaced trees and low brush in the daylight took on a sinister edge in the night. I craved a path, but was trapped in a wall-less labyrinth of trees. I could walk easily in any direction. But in darkness all directions were the same. When I walked ahead, the trees around me all seemed identical. Moving, I did not move. I had no reference, no way to mark progress. It was all very disconcerting. It's hard to explain, but I can still recall the panic. It was a relief to plunge back into the familiar tangle pine and vine. Then, a clear patch, a brief respite and I stumbled ahead a yard or so and plunged back in to the density of cruel vines and twigs. Their malevolence was actual to me. They were living creatures, venom in their sinews. And if you think that plants can't hate, these could, and this was their chance. The ruined house and the wall and the tire, I knew why the people left, the plants at night tore them. And for a few moments, I think back now, I was insane. And my insane brain took time to understand the meaning of the respite I had stumbled across. I went back. Had I crossed a road? A road, yes. I turned to follow it. Which way? I wanted south. Maybe it was the road to the cabin? I couldn't tell. I didn't care any longer. It was something to follow, and I would follow it. Even if it didn't lead to the camp and the cabin and the old man, at least it led somewhere. I had figured it out and felt better. My panic subsided. I just had to follow the road.

I felt relief on the road but walked fast, felt foolish for the panic. *On the Road* I nervously laughed to myself. A downed tree across my path, I almost stumbled. Its broken branches had become spikes, some standing upright. If I had fallen on it I could have been impaled. I shivered. It was all I could do to not run. Ahead I saw another deer. No, a dog. A big dog. Dog as big as a deer. Had it been watching me all along? The other deer? Had they been dogs? No, I had seen them clearly. This was the doberman, and he stood his ground and snarled at me. He had stepped out from the brush. He didn't bark. He remembered me. He had the upper hand. The shepherd came out and stopped, then the line of puppies came across from one side of the road to the other. Mom growled low as she went by. She remembered me too. And behind me I could hear the rustles of the others. They were surrounding me. No thick branches for a club, worthless trees too thin to climb, brittle, ineffectual twigs. I didn't know what to do. Waited, fully expecting a confederate to leap at me from behind. I felt the malice of a cruel nature in this pack of beasts, anticipating revenge for invading their haven. It was as if all the evil of the world stood between me and my goal. I remained still, like the fawn, while they moved on. The doberman, the shepherd, the puppies, the others vanished into the trees. All they wanted was to cross the road, to follow the single-track trail to their home. The only malice was in my own mind.

Home? Were they headed home? Did they know the way? They must.

I turned onto the trail that they had taken. It made all the sense in the world to stay on the road, but I turned to the forest to follow the path of feral dogs. I kept well back. Stopped to listen for them. Would they know I was following them? Did they care? As I moved slowly through the brush I could just pick up the trail. All but a few feet ahead was indistinct or just plain, impenetrable dark. But close I could see the dips in the ground and the fallen trees and even the punishing twigs. I calmed and didn't care and walked on. I had surrendered to simply walk to wherever it led.

I saw his fire. When I paused I heard softly,
"What do ya do with a drunken sailor?
"What do ya do with a drunken sailor?
"What do ya do with a drunken sailor?

# the spark of life

"Put 'im in a bunk with the bishop's daughter,
"Put 'im in a bunk with the bishop's daughter,
"Put 'im in a bunk with the bishop's daughter,
"Leave 'em till the Lord converts her."
The old man grinned, "Where ya been? Thought ya ran out. Wouldn't be the first, ya ..."
He stopped when I stepped into the light and got a good look at my ripped shirt, torn cheek.
"You been out fighting Bigfoot?" He laughed not a joyous laugh. I wiped my cheek and knocked off the nascent scab. The back of my hand was again bloodied. "What happened to ya?"
"Nothing.
"Stickers.
"A scratch."
"Look like you run into that ol' Devil. Jersey Devil got ya?
"Look what *I* got ya." He moved to the shore and held up a string of small, disc-shaped fish. Seven wet, black bodies glimmered in the firelight.
"I'm not hungry."
Harry put the fish down slowly. "Maybe later?"
"I need a drink."
"Gone. Done," he practically shouted. "Done gone. On the wagon. Fresh start. Thought you was gone for good. Sorry. Woulda left ya some. Only a sip left anyway." He held up the pint that had held vodka. I

recognized his emergency stash. He turned it upside down to show it was empty, then, "Bombs away," flung toward the lake. Splash in the night. "Plenty when the wine's done. Got to clean ourselves out a bit. Get the old web out of the cobs. Rest and re-coop-er-ate," said as if he were speaking the lines of a play. "Take a little ride on the water wagon."

So he was on the wagon. Asshole. He had more. Somewhere. He was drunk and too happy to have really run out. Had he finished the booze in the canteen? Probably not. Drunks always have a little stash somewhere—until they don't. Well, I had my little stash too—the fifth in the rubbish pile. He wouldn't have found that. I picked a burning stick for a torch and headed behind the boathouse.

"Where ya going?"

My torch was little help, all but extinguishing itself as soon as it was away from the heat of the fire. I stumbled, tried to go slowly and not hurt myself. A rusty cut, to fall and slice an artery, nobody would ever know what happened to me. I couldn't imagine the old drunk being able to help.

"Come back here." I heard him in the background. "Bigfoot's out there. Them dogs too! We'll drink the wine. Jersey Devil. I seen him. Might be I can find us something. Don't leave me." The thought of being alone was too much for Harry. He'd even trade his booze for company. But he wouldn't need to. I found the fifth. I considered taking a swig and leaving the bottle—not telling Harry, saying that I just had to take a piss. I was *very* careful now that I had the bottle in my hands.

"What ya got there, son? That what I think it is?"

It was good Scotch, the real deal, sealed with a cork. I took a long drink and handed it to Harry. He took a long drink also and smiled.

"I got ya some fish," he hazarded. "We's ah team. Right? I got them fish?"

It was too soon. The whiskey hadn't hit me yet. I waved him off and took another pull on the bottle, handed it to Harry. He took a cautious pull, feeling me out and gauging my anger. I took it back and put the cork in. It was my bottle. I could do with it what I wanted.

Harry talked, "I been studying on it, this camp here. Tomorrow we clean some of them trees out. Make it presentable. I'm thinking we stake a claim. Nobody's land. Nobody owns it maybe. Maybe some widow, bad memories for her. Back taxes and all. She'd help us out. Cleaning up drunks. That's her good Christian duty." Harry was captivated by the idea of turning the old camp into a drunk farm, raising drunks.

"Raising drunks to be men." He could take the simplest idea, something that had popped into his head, and make it into a story. He lived in a world of improbable stories. He made sense of the chaos of his life by turning it all into a series of narratives—private myths that explained and comforted and gave him the will to face each day—like that day's idea that some widow owned the land, and this "Christian widow" would help us because her "drunk of a dead husband" who had established this camp would "in his blessed memory" help Harry and me start a drunk farm, on which we would raise drunks like farmer Jones raises corn. Harry was full of great ideas, barstool ideas, crazy shit, just plausible enough to make one pause. "She's bankrolling the whole thing. She's a good woman. You can talk to her. College boy an' all, you know how to talk to her. Tell her how this here camp did turn my life around. Made me a good Christian man."

I didn't want to hear it. I got up. Took the bottle. It was mine. I found it. And went to the cabin.

"Where you off to?" Harry called.

"Change my shirt."

I lit a match to find my way, then lit the lantern off it. I put the Scotch next to it. There was a white dress shirt hanging in the bunk room. I noted that my rucksack had been upended and emptied on the bed. Asshole. But I wasn't angry. He couldn't help it. He was an old drunk. The booze had hit me, and I was charitable. I tried the shirt on. It fit. I looked at my face in the mirror. Cut and blood on my cheek, stubble on my chin. Dirty too. I needed to clean myself.

"Hoo-ray and up she rises,

"Hoo-ray and up she rises,

"Hoo-ray and up she rises,

"Earle-eye in the morning."

I walked past Harry's singing and away from the fire's comforting womb of light, rested on my knees in the wet sand, splashed my face with the cold water. I cupped my hands and brought more over my head and let it fall through my fingers, looked upwards to stars overhead, fell slowly on my back. I saw more stars than I had seen forever. Had I ever been away from the city's light? Really looked into the night? It was overwhelming. I saw what I supposed was the Milky Way. Was it possible that they were all stars?

Suns burning, with planets and ... what? And the Milky Way was just the beginning. Some of those stars were galaxies, more Milky Ways. On into infinity? No, they were finite. They stopped somewhere. I could count them. Infinity was easy. Infinity was unimaginable by definition. My mind could rest in the infinite, stop trying to imagine. No point. But these stars, I could count them if I had the time. Finite made them more profound, and more frightening. They were fires burning in the night. Burning till they were gone.

I got up to find the bottle. Where was it? I had left it in the cabin. I was feeling it. I wanted more.

Harry was looking into the fire, singing softly his stupid song,

"What do ya do with a drunken sailor?

"What do ya do with a drunken sailor?

"What do ya do with a drunken sailor?"

I got the bottle and sat next to Harry. Took a sip, handed it to him.

"Do you want them fish?" Harry asked quietly.

"Not really."

"They's just fish. It's okay. It's just the way things are. Ya done your best, son."

"I'm not hungry." But I *was* hungry.

"I'll show ya how to make 'em up. Make 'em up hobo style, an old drunk taught me when I's just a boy," he smiled and winked. "Jus' like you." With the right level of alcohol flowing through his brain, Harry was an accomplished roadside woodsman. He had some fish gutted and cleaned and skewered on sticks in a couple of minutes. "Just roast 'em like a marshmallow. Don't cook 'em too long."

We ate without utensils, pulling off flesh with our fingers. He was a drunk and a bum and a loser and all that, but Harry wasn't a bad man, and he wasn't a fool. He sensed my disquietude and wanted to help. "Fish is meant to be eaten. Jesus made 'em that way. Remember, Jesus give the multitude fish and wine."

In the intervening years, one of the things that *has* changed about me is that I no longer try to win people over to my point of view. Accuse me of cynicism, nihilism, apathy, ennui, not giving a shit. (Now it isn't as if I wouldn't pull you back if I saw you stepping into the path of a train. And if you insisted on stepping again onto the tracks, I would *not* now try to dissuade you, but I would quietly wait and pull you back. Again and again if need be.) But proselytizing? No, not anymore, not me. You figure it out. Today I live in the forest. *You* have to figure it out for yourself. All I can tell you is what happened to me, as truly as I can. But on that unseasonably-warm spring night of my youth, the Logos was my Gospel, and I was the Apostle of Reason. And I was just drunk enough to save Harry from Jesus.

"I've had my fill of Jesus. A fairy tale, like Santa Claus, for people who can't face reality," and I proceeded to march out all the well-worn arguments against religion— war, prejudice, vainglory, preposterous science, the Spanish Inquisition, the Children's Crusade, the Pope's Oyster Pearl Rolex. My apostasy was personal, and I was going to tell Harry all about it. And Harry—he didn't know what hit him.

"When I was sixteen (An aeon ago when I was twenty-two, just yesterday now that I'm almost sixty.) I went on a weekend retreat. We went up to this camp in the Poconos," I told him. "There was a bunch of kids from my church and kids from other churches and these Jesus freaks who put on the show. It was all about getting saved.

"And I met a pretty girl. She was older than me. She had long brown, hair, pulled back loose. She wore this white, peasant blouse. She played guitar and sang that first night, and we took a walk afterwards, in the woods along a stream, and she told me about her Jesus.

"But her Jesus was a new Jesus. He wasn't the Jesus I had known from my childhood, the one from my church and my family. Mine was the Jesus of Love. 'Children come unto me.' My Jesus took care of me. He taught me to be kind and open and to trust and to love the world with open arms and help the poor. He was the Jesus of my mother who called the bums on Vine Street 'unfortunates,' and when a neighbor was hospitalized my mother cooked meals so sons and husband would have hot, home-cooked nourishment. That was my mother's Jesus. Maybe I hadn't been listening too closely at church, because this girl had another one.

"She told me that you had to give yourself to Him to be saved. Everybody else was going to Hell. You could be the nicest person in the world, but if you didn't ask Him into your life, you were doomed. I had a lot of questions, like, 'What happens to people who never have that chance? Do they go to Hell? I mean, if you need Jesus to be saved, what about the ones who never hear about Him?' I wanted to know about the Jews and the Chinese and Africans and all the rest. She just said, 'That's why we have missionaries. That's why we witness. That's why we love Jesus.' Not even the Catholics were going to Heaven unless they turned to Jesus. And the Pope? He was going to the darkest, hottest Hell. It seemed to me that Hell was going to be pretty crowded. 'Even my mom?' And I remember this girl's face as she said this, unless my mom accepted Jesus into her life, 'Off the Hell she'll go. That's why it's so important that she gets down on her knees and prays to Jesus.'"

I hear Harry's cry breaking in, "Ain't no man's momma going to Hell. My sainted momma took me in every time. Every time. Always had a dollar in her apron to buy her boy a pint. Help her son get through the day. Bless her soul, used to say, 'World's a brighter place when you got a dollar in your pocket.'"

Now, half-a-lifetime later as I write this, I see this girl's face as she matter-of-factly condemns my mother to eternal damnation. I see the white, peasant blouse and her dogmatic smile—but I begin to understand. Many years removed from the girl and from Harry and my own fight with the bottle, I look back and understand that there *is* a powerful truth hidden in her message. But to make it manifest, as she did with *her* Jesus, is to put it in a cage. Limit it, define it—make it definite, finite—you get this girl in the blouse and her cruel damnation. No. Words must fail, narrative fail also, and so fail image and intellect. To try and say what *It* is … it's like grabbing a fistful of mud from the bottom of the lake—death and decay and life reborn squeezed through ineffectual fingers. But there *is* something there, the pungent miasma of some truth remains. It's what Jack and all the others were looking for. What I was looking for.

"So," I continued. "So the next day she sought me out. And we walked along the little stream, and we talked. We sat on the bank, and she played guitar and sang beautiful songs about Armageddon and the Apocalypse. 'You're going to Hell,' she said sweetly. 'Don't go to Hell. We can be in Heaven together.' But I couldn't. Not yet.

"That night, Saturday night," they had a guy preaching. He had long, blond hair, pulled back in a ponytail, wore faded jeans with neatly-done patches, and he was really clean. I remember thinking how clean and creased his jeans and shirt were. So, it's Saturday night, after singing and preaching and kids sharing their stories and more singing with the pretty girl singing and two guys with electric guitars, this preacher guy looks at his watch. Calls out, 'Jesus be praised. It's midnight. It's Sunday. The day of the Lord. Who will come forward and be saved in His name.'

"It was an altar call, asking for people to come up and dedicate their lives to Jesus.

"Sitting here in the woods, telling you about it, it sounds nuts. But it was intense. In college I've read about brainwashing, that's what it was. Peer pressure. But I held back."

Harry broke in, "Contrary nature, son. You got a nature that's contrary. Contrary man myself. Tell me up, I'll tell you down. Point right, I look left. Watch your back. Back to front. I seen them hallelujah boys working. I know what you seen. Seen what you know … pass me that bottle, son."

"I held back," I continued. "More and more people, kids that I had grown up with, went forward and everyone clapped and cheered as they got on their knees and raised their arms to Jesus. But I held back. I held back. I didn't feel it. I thought the other's did. I couldn't proclaim. So I didn't go up. I almost did, but I didn't."

"You got that bottle there?"

"So. So things got nuts. A girl, I grew up with her. We went to school together since kindergarten. I could see her backyard from mine. Her dad built a tire rope-swing that I used to play on. She had a golden retriever named Sam that used to get loose and come to our backdoor. My mom would give him cookies.

"She stood and held her hands up and shook them and started screaming, 'Jesus Jesus Jesus Jesus,' with tears and sobbing. Then another girl from some other town, a different girl, I didn't know her, she did the same thing, hands in the air, sobbing, 'Jesus Christ Jesus Jesus Lord in Heaven Lord in Heaven.' Some guy standing right beside me, 'Jesus Christ ... Lord of Heaven ... save me! Save me! Save me! Son of God!'

"We'd been sitting, but now we were standing. A couple of guys in front of me upset their chairs when they jumped up. I stood because everyone else did. Some girl stood on her chair, and it folded back on her, and a boy caught her. They were all hugging each other and crying and laughing and all together. Just one big knot of kids. Then, suddenly, the preacher was waving his arms and lifting his legs way up in this funny dance and then went charging down the aisle. Others started doing the same thing, running around like headless chickens."

"I seen a headless chicken once. At the state fair or someplace," Harry added helpfully. "George, or Gary, or Molly the Headless Chicken ... naw ... what was its name again?"

"There wasn't a chicken," I said exasperated. "Don't be stupid. Pay attention."

"Don't mind. Ain't got to be mean. Don't be getting all bent up. Say, where's that bottle got to?"

"They're all dancing around. Except the pretty girl, she was up front, standing off to the side. And I wasn't dancing. I had my back up against the wall. People had their hands up in the air. I'm standing in the back, and I'm looking for the girl, but I can't see through the knot of kids dancing in the center ... and the preacher raises his hands to God and Jesus and the Holy Ghost ... 'I feel the Holy ... the Holy Ghost has entered my soul, the Holy Ghost. Jesus commands. Jesus commands me to speak.'"

"Knew a man, bite the head off a chicken. Carnival geek he was."

"No. No chickens. He was shouting gibberish. It sounded like, I don't know, it wasn't like French or Spanish, those are the only languages I've ever heard. Maybe Russian, or Arabic. It was weird and guttural. Others started doing it. Some were just making noises, like 'woo woo woo woo.' But the preacher was really good at it. I closed my eyes and prayed and wanted to feel the Holy Ghost and Jesus and God enter my soul, but I didn't feel anything. I tried. I really tried. But nothing.

"I opened my eyes. I'm watching the preacher. He's just standing there with a big grin watching it all. I watch him walk over and pick up one of the electric guitars and plug it into the amp, and he turns it up and starts to strum. He gets back on the microphone and says real soft, but with the mic turned up so it's a booming whisper and the guitar's coming out in the background. 'Our Father who art in Heaven ...'

"You know the rest. The kids quieted down, and it was over.

"I walked down to the stream and sat and didn't know what to think. I wondered if I had missed something profound. I wanted that girl to find me and be with me. I wanted to give my life to Jesus, to do it quietly and secretly. But I didn't feel anything. Was I a sinner and doomed? And when Jesus came and took everyone to Paradise, would I be forever alone?"

"Ain't you getting a little dry with all that talking?"

"Here. Take it." I gave him the bottle and went on. "Driving home, the next day, in Mrs. Machalski's station wagon, the neighbor girl asked if I'd been saved. I told her I had. Maybe it was a lie. Maybe not? I'd tried. Tried to ask Him into me. She hugged me and cried a little."

"Here ya go." Harry held out the bottle.

"I felt awful, like everyone else had gotten a present or something and I didn't. But nothing changed. In school they were just the same. It wasn't like they had all turned into saints or something. It was a cheat. A fraud. A fiction ...

"a make-believe."

"Mike. Mike's his name."

"Whose name?"

"Headless chicken's. Chicken's Mike. Mike weren't no make-believe. I saw him with my own eyes. Steel Pier, that's where he was. Nation's Playground. Playground of the Nation. Atlantic Ocean. Ain't no jokin'."

"Harry, what the hell?"

"My daddy, on my birthday, daddy took me and some of the boys in the neighborhood, boys like me, my friends, loaded us in the car. Daddy had a big, blue Oldsmobile then. My father's Oldsmobile. Off to Atlantic City we'd go. Off to Steel Pier. My daddy say we gonna spend a hundred dollars for my birthday. Won it at the track. Big money. 'Today our budget's one hundred dollars,' my daddy'd say. And we'd say, 'Yay.' 'And we're gonna spend every penny of it.' And we'd say, 'Hooray.' That's where he was, Steel Pier, Mike the Headless Wonder, chicken he was. Man who owned him fed him with an eyedropper. I saw him. He was alive, walking 'round. Not one of them pickled punks, babies with three eyes, cows with one horn, lambs with two heads where you can see the stitches holding 'em together. He was walking 'round the stage and all. Alive as you and me."

"Harry, I was talking about Jesus and God."

"Wonder what happened to him. If you ain't got no head, you can't never die ...

"... can you?"

"I don't know. How could it not have a head? How did it eat?"

"Told ya, man fed him with an eyedropper."

"How did it see?"

"Blind man gets around. Blind man don't see with his eyes. Same thing.

"Tell me a chicken without a head ain't got no soul," continued Harry with *his* lesson in theology.

"What kind of God lets a poor chicken live without a head? What's the point?"

Harry paused me, "Maybe's to make that man who owned him rich. Man works his life raising chickens. Picking up eggs. Chopping off heads. God says, 'You're a hard-working man. I'm making you rich. See the world. You and that chicken.'"

"He didn't have any head. The chicken couldn't see."

"Not the chicken. The man, man saw the world."

"Why didn't God just let the man find a big diamond on the ground? Save the chicken its agony."

"Don't work that way with God. 'God works in *mysterious* ways.' You never heard that?"

"Harry, that's the stupidest thing I ever heard in my life."

"Don't be getting all bent on me. Take a drink. I'll have one. Youse a college boy. Tell me. That chicken. You think its soul went to Heaven when it got its head chopped off. Or did the soul stay until the body died?"

"You said it couldn't die. You said that if it didn't have a head it couldn't die." I had him, tripped him up with his own crazy logic.

"WooWee, you sure is a college boy. No beating you. Got me. Got me good. But let's say he does die. When does he go to Heaven?"

"Maybe he went to Hell. Maybe he didn't ask chicken Jesus to come into his chicken life."

"Rooster Jesus. Jesus would be a rooster I believe," Harry explained. "The head. That would be dead when they chopped it off. Did that head's soul go to Heaven? And the body, that's still going, till it's dead. Did it have a soul?"

"Maybe it has two souls. Maybe has half a soul in its head and half in its body, and God reunites them when the body dies," I said.

"There ya go son. Scholarship at its best. Youse good at figuring."

"Animals don't go to Heaven," I added.

"Why not?"

"They're animals."

"Well they should. More than people. Animal never hurt nobody without a reason. Not like a man. Man'll kick ya just to watch you cry. Laugh to watch you bleed."

"Nobody goes to Heaven, Harry. Not animals. Not people."

"Had a dog that used to water ski. German shepherd as I recall, same kinda dog that's been sniffing 'round here. Maybe we could teach him. Steel Pier, had a speed boat speeding by. Man says, 'Look over there, the Water Skiing Dog.' Made my daddy laugh. My daddy didn't laugh at much. Don't remember my daddy laughing much. I remember like it was yesterday, daddy tossing his head back, laughing good at that dog."

I didn't know what to say.

"I knew a man a long time ago who bit the heads off chickens. He'd bite the head off a snake. Rats. Mice. Corn dogs. This man would eat anything for a drink. Saw him eat a  spider for a shot of rye. Mostly rats. He kinda specialized in rats. He was a good rat catcher. 'Ya can always find a rat on the Row,' he says. He'd walk into a bar with a rat in his hand an' say, 'Set me up. I'm gonna bite the head off-ah this rat.' And he would! Cowboy set him up. Who'd do that? Why not just buy a man a drink? Face was all tored up from the rats. Rats used to fight back. Bite him and he'd bite their heads off. Least that's what he said they done. Don't know, maybe had his face bit when he was sleeping one off. Or he maybe froze it off in the cold. That man hated them rats. Maybe something happened when he was child? Ya think? Froze to death in the end. Froze 'is toes. Froze 'is nose. Took him into the hospital myself. Carried him on my back. Never come out. Had a pint in his pocket. Froze solid. He was my friend.

"Saw a geek biting heads off chickens when I was a boy. Daddy'd take us boys to the Pier for my birthday. Had him in a pit down a side street. He was all dirty. Hair matted, long. Howling and ah shaking. Had a brown stain on the butt of his pants. Sad thing for a boy to see. Free to see. Just look into the pit. Mercy. Mercy me. Daddy called us boys back, but it was too late. I seen it. Man was selling chickens. People buy a chicken to throw in the pit. Poor sonofabitch bites its head off. That's how he made his dough, selling them chickens. Probably sold 'em again to the restaurant next door, eh? How'd you like to know you'd be eating a drumstick from some ol' hen that had its head bit off?

"All dressed up. That's how I remember 'em. Men with hats and ladies with gloves, buying them chickens. People use to dress up then. Never saw my daddy leave the house without his hat. Wonder what's worse? Biting off them heads or buying them chickens and watching 'em. Sad thing."

"Give me that bottle," I said, and I took a swig. I looked through the whiskey we had left and into the flames of our fire.

I saw Harry watching it. "We still got that wine," he said. I didn't realize at the time how serious it was for Harry to run out. I had no idea what was coming.

"I seen it too," Harry said. "About them Jesus freaks.

"I seen men find Jesus."

"Men just like me. Drunks! One day they're drinking, and the next day they're preaching at ya. I saw a fellow, dead man, been in the ground for a decade. Rose from the dead," Harry said, lifting his arms and shaking his voice like an old-time preacher. "Walked up to me an' held out his paw. 'Harry?' he says. Ugly sonofabitch. Shake his hand I did. Soft as putty. Man-e-cured. Nails all done up. I look him over, and I maybe can remember him, like somebody's brother. Nose all scarred up like I could almost know.

"'Harry,' he says and puts out his paw. 'It's Jack. Don't you remember me, Harry? I remember you. You gave me your pint one night when I was having the shakes. Took me to the hospital when I was frozen. I had hypothermia. I would have died except for that bottle you gave me. You carried me on your back.'

"'You ain't him,' I said. 'You can't be him. Jack's dead. Jack's in a box. Jack's six feet down. In the ground. What ya want with me?'

"'I just want to say hello, Harry. And thank you. And tell you I'm sorry for all the times I crossed you.'

"'You ain't him! You don't look like him! You ain't dressed like him. That your car? He got no car. Just like me. I remember Jack. Jack was a stinking, hopeless drunk. In the ground. In a box.'

"Jack in the box. Jack in the box. Get it?"

"I get it," I said.

"So I says, 'You got a hundred dollars? If you're him give me some. You owe me that pint. With interest!'

"'I got religion, Harry. I'm not drinking anymore.' Man trying to preach to me. Like that girl doing to you. 'I found my God, found Him in an empty bottle.'

"'You got nothing. Get away. Ain't nothing in an empty bottle. Jack's dead. Froze his toes off on a railroad track. Carried him to the hospital myself. Seen 'em cut the toes off his foot. Snip. Snip. Snip. Jack's dead. Froze in Denver. Never come out. Frozen dead he was.'

"That's what I said," Harry told me. "And damn if that man didn't sit right there on the stinking curb in his nice suit and take off his nice shoe and take off his nice, silk sock.

"And he ain't got no toes!

"JesusMaryJoseph. I look at his eyes again, and it's Jack! And I say, 'You own me for that. I saved your stinking life. You give me a hundred bucks and we'll call it even. Jesus says to help the poor, right? Jesus had a hundred bucks, He'd help a man out. Fed them peoples with them fish and loaves and wine. Right? Jesus give ya money. Give ya the shirt off His back. Jesus give ya a bottle. Tell ya what this damn sonofabitch gave me.

"He takes out his roll, and he's got bills and bills and big ones on top, and he peels off a bill and hands it to me.

"And I'm ah shakin' so I can hardly see it. And I can't see it, and he knows it.

"'It's a ten Harry. If I gave you more, somebody'd knock you on the head for it. Or you'd drink yourself to death.'

"I knew them scars. Knew 'em. It was him. Man back from the dead. Dead man reborn. Takes a drunk to know a drunk. Jack, here he was. Saved by Jesus."

"There's no Jesus," I said.

"Man stopped his drinking. That's something. Something! Something going on there."

"It doesn't mean it was Jesus."

"Man wanted a drink so bad he had his face bit by rats. Something going on."

"He simply decided," I said, "that enough was enough. He got tired of having to bite the heads off rats and chickens and whatever, and he decided to stop drinking and get a job."

"It ain't that easy."

"What's not that easy?"

"Drinking boy. Not Drinking. Ain't that easy to stop drinking."

"It's just will power. You just stop. Get a job. Get on with your life."

"Ain't that easy. Hell, if it was that easy, be no drunks. You wait. You'll see ..."

He turned his head away, looked into the fire. "I'm gonna do it this time. Stopping my drinking. Taking a break here at this farm we got."

"You gonna find Jesus?" I asked cynically.

"Maybe. May ... be He finds me ...

"... may ... be, He finds you."

"I got my Jesus right here," I said and took a big, drunken, sacrilegious swig. Harry's little story sounded too perfect, something the proselytizers would say, a poignant, well-formed fiction. Chicken without a head. Man without toes. I had to tell him. Make it clear and pound it home. I could tell he was weakening, almost disbelieving. "It's fraud," I said. "People believe it. But it's fraud. Look at the sky, stars and stars, night after night. People can't stand it. It's too big. Too frightening. We need a story.

"Look." I took a torch from the flames and stood and walked over to the shore and plunged its fire into the lake. I waved the wet stick in Harry's face.

"Where's the fire?

"Does the fire go to Heaven?

"Does the fire have a soul?

"I don't know."

"It called redox. Reduction/oxidation. It's combustion. A simple chemical reaction. It's oxygen combining with carbon and other shit to make energy. To make heat. To make fire. To make life. And inside you, inside me, inside every cell is slow fire burning oxygen and making heat, energy to keep you moving. That's why you sweat. That's why you stay warm. That's why you to have to eat, to breathe. It's fuel. It's fire burning inside you. Thinking that you and me and everyone else is more that just a speck of carbon burning on a stick—it's just a trick. A story. We're nothing but a chemical reaction. It's neurons firing in your brain. All the thinking, it helps us survive better, but it doesn't mean that we have a soul or that we're going to Heaven or Jesus is going to save us.

"A billion years ago a lightning spark came down and hit a lake like this one. That spark ignited the fire, and we call it life. And it's been catching on to stuff since then. Like a match lighting a candle. Lighting a million candles. But when it's done it's done. And it's nothing. Nothing left."

"So why? Tell me there's no God. Why are we here then? If they ain't no God."

"We're here for the same reason the rocks and the trees and the dogs and the … the … fire is here."

"What reason is that?"

"No reason at all."

"That's awful depressing," Harry sighed.

"Exactly! That's it! That's why we have God! If it wasn't for God and Heaven and some reason for all this, life would be so God damn depressing that we'd all just lie down and die." I handed it to Harry. "Life. A wet, dead stick.

"Give me the bottle."

I felt the triumph of finally breaking him down. He looked crestfallen. I'd convinced him. There was no God. No Heaven. No point. No hope.

"How do ya expect a man to stop drinking when you go talking like that?"

"Voltaire said, 'If there wasn't a God, man would have to invent Him.'

"It's all crap."

"Why you got to be so mean?"

"Because that's the way it is. It's all a trick. The fire goes out and you're gone."

Harry took the stick and stuck it in the fire. It popped and sizzled. Sparks flew from it, and after a time the fire took hold, and Harry held it up, then handed it to me. He walked back to the lake and picked up the last of the fish, cold and dead and still on the stringer. He waved it in my direction.

"Ain't no fire. Only Jesus bring this fish back to life."

I was dumbfounded. I had used that example dozens of times. In coffee shops and bars—a match, blowing it out with a dramatic, "There. There's your life. Tell me a match has a soul." No one had ever done what Harry had done. He'd brought it back to life, so to speak, and damned my analogy. I could see that my logic was futile.

I looked at my bottle in the firelight. "It's almost gone." I took a swig, careful not to take too much, and handed it back to Harry. He looked through it in the firelight and set it down between his legs. There was only about an inch left. When it was gone, it would be gone. So long as there was that inch, there was hope.

"Them dogs? They thinking about God? They got religion? Do they? What ya think they think? Dogs got a God?"

"Xenophanes said that if a dog had a God, it would look like a dog."

"Who?"

"Some old Greek. It doesn't matter. He's dead."

"We gonna be the God of dogs. You give me a hand."

"The what?"

"Manna boy. Manna from Heaven. Loafs and fishes.

"Gonna save them wild dogs.

"Gonna be Jesus of the hounds.

"Can't have 'em running 'round chasing the drunks. Man's best friend ya know ... a dog. Drunks and dogs. Gotta make friends with 'em. Gonna be a God among dogs. Here, give me a hand."

"'If there *is* a God," I thought. "We're both going to Hell."

Harry had the plan. We were going to feed the dogs and make them our friends. Perhaps even teach the shepherd to water ski. We banged about in the boathouse with the lantern and tore into boxes and crates of rations. "Kill 'em or cure 'em. Either way we win!" Harry laughed. He liked his drunken plan, and it made him feel good to be carrying it out. He had some booze in him and didn't want to let the good feeling go. He wanted to remember that there was more to the world than frozen toes and geeks in pits and well-dressed gentleman and ladies who would pay to watch a diseased man degrade himself. The fifth by the fire with his inch was waiting for him. I eyed it, but did not touch it. In later years I would play the same trick with myself, leaving a taste as long as I could, maybe to prove something to myself, maybe because running out was so awful.

"Smells about right for dog food," I said. Harry started to put the cans out, but I was concerned that the peeled-open cans had sharp edges. "They're going to cut themselves. We need to dish it out," I said.

"Get some dishes," Harry commanded.

"Fine." I did. I was pretty loaded. The whole thing was a lark. We filled the bowls by the firelight and set them out by the boathouse at the edge of the light. The dogs rustled around in the woods unseen. We watched. Cerberus came out first—I had named the doberman. I saw his nose in the light. He sniffed, but when Harry stood and called to him to eat, the wary pooch dashed back into his darkness. The shepherd, now dubbed by Harry, Rin Tin Tin, ran across the front of the cabin, a quick dash, the shadow of an ancient memory to surround prey. A hairy compadre followed, looking like it'd lived feral for a long time, loped with a limp. "Old Man, I got some food," Harry called after the disappearing mutt.

Nobody was taking the bait. "We've got to it put in the woods. It's too close to the fire," I said.

"Then we can't see 'em," Harry countered.

"It doesn't matter if we see them." But I knew it did. We wanted to watch them eat our charity. Meanwhile I kept opening cans. Harry fumbled, breaking off tabs.

"I need more plates and bowls," he said, turning now to scooping out the contents of the cans I had liberated.

"You hungry? Heat some up?" I asked. Harry licked his finger and nodded. I got some bowls from the cabin and took up the cooking pot, added some water from the lake, and Harry threw in some handfuls of gruel. The pooches still weren't buying into our providence. I put out more food and pushed it into the trees. In the pause while our food heated, I looked at the bottle again, but it was right next to him, and by rights was his, still with an inch. I lit an old ration-smoke and felt my head spin. The pups came out first, waiting I suppose for our motion to desist before venturing forth. Mom came out behind them. "Snow White and the Seven Dwarfs ... Grumpy, Happy, Sad, Fatty, ..." Harry's voice trailed off. He didn't know them all, neither did I.

"More like the Seven Deadly Sins," I said. "Sloth, Avarice, Greed, Hate, Prejudice, Lying, ..." I didn't know, couldn't think of them.

"Drinking," Harry added. "Running Dry." His mind was never far from running out. Even with a full bottle, after that first sip, running out's on your mind.

"We'll call 'em the days of the week. Hell boy. I know's them. What's today?"

Cerberus came out, looked at us, then ate greedily. Rin Tin Tin was next, trailed by a  handsome hound with a collar, we called it Huckleberry. Old Man pushed his way in past the pups, giving them a growl. One dog I couldn't quite make out held back in the woods. Scruffy Terror came out warily, then retreated. I took some handfuls, made them into meatballs, threw them as far as I could into the trees. Maybe others were out there? I was losing track. Harry scooped up a handful of the *Meat Stew* glop and walked toward Snow White. "Have her eating out of my hand," he said. She didn't approve and made it clear that Harry should retreat. He put the glop on the sand and moved carefully back. "Might take a couple of days. Making friends."

"Or a couple of generations."

Naming the dogs brought them into our world. From a pack of amorphous creatures they became compadres. The dogs didn't know we had named them, so nothing changed for them. But for us, to name a thing is to think that we know it. And with our naming of them, the dogs became players in this story we were creating from chaos.

Harry finished the booze in a gulp.

"Man overboard."

The last bottle splashed into the dark lake.

# to God in anger

I sit on an empty Atlantic beach, beat and broken. Kerouac is dead—on his knees hemorrhaging into a toilet bowl. Cassidy too—on a lonely railroad right-of-way. Poets' leaves scattered to the wind. Snyder teaching college. Ginsberg survives in his poems—charming old man, plays the harmonium, and we all chant before tramping through Camden to visit Walt's house. And Avalokiteśvara, where has he gone off to? Off to Nirvana at last? Who knows? A dream of youth? Maybe listening now?

In an attic-box I find my back-broken copy of *On The Road*. The cold sea breeze blows the pages free while I sit on the beach. I chase them down. The whole thing threatens to fall apart. I keep it together with a rubber band. *The Road*—a lifetime since I touched its pages. I shake my head, reading in wonder of myself and how this ever could have become a model for my life. I see the trail of wreckage left behind—broken promises, lovers betrayed, fatherless children, orphaned mothers, fallen angels, death. I am disappointed. These men are the heroes of my youth. Too young and too hurried to read Thoreau, I take my lessons from Jack and Neal and Gary and Alan. These are my aspirations—independence, enlightenment, road trips, parties, Zen, jazz, poetry, truth, Tuesday groves of redwoods and, of course, the naked nymphs. I am just a kid trying to live the Romance. Literature, not experience my guide. I mistake illusion for essence, don't have the background to read between the lines.

But I *had* done it.

Under Jack's tutelage, I drink the sweet port he favored. Switch to whiskey when the port stops working. I get stinking drunk at inopportune moments. Swat bugs beneath solitary street lamps. I sleep under a broad sky, barely hidden in a shallow ditch on an open prairie. Sleep warm and wake to frost on my sleeping bag. On a distant farm I see a lone pine lit for Christmas with multi-colored bulbs, far, far from my home. I read the *Diamond Sutra* and do my best to believe every word. Meditate. Hitchhike from here to nowhere, hop freights, sleep in fleabag hotels, wake to mouse-chewed shoes, kiss dark women in doorways darker still. And always, in every holy alley, look for my Alan, my Gary, my Neal, my Jack, my bodhisattva—a glimpse disappearing around a corner, a shadow in the shadows, a solo that lifts my soul—I am so close.

I believe in the promise of *The Road.* I look for my destination, until the looking becomes the thing itself. I learn soon enough that hard times are easy in print, not so in life. That on the highway, late and alone, cold and rain and sleet are no bodhisattva illusion. That suffering is real. But I learn also that it is *only* suffering, only cold and only rain and only sleet and that there is compassion in the downshifting 18-wheeler. And that while the big rig's high beams burn a tunnel in the night, my world is a tunnel of my own making. Is that what Jack is trying to tell me? And there, on the shoulder, in the darkness, does Avalokiteśvara watch me pass?

Maybe?

Jack insists that beyond the Beat is Beatitude. That this life is an illusion, a tunnel in the darkness, and real is something beyond. Jack writes that he has his satori and finds enlightenment on Desolation Peak. Yet he dies a bitter drunk. Is he lying to me? To himself? That's what I don't understand. What happens? Why does Jack leave the mountain and return to the weed and the women and the booze? And why the bitterness? How does my hero finish out his life as a cranky, middle-aged drunk? Angry at the world, yells all day at the TV, estranged from all he loves and still loves him.

And still I follow my Gospel. I wail in the night, running, searching, climbing, louder, faster, higher. Suddenly it seems around some corner I'm on the Row. Not physically perhaps, but spiritually and truly. And my adventure is a sad, drunken revelry of all the roads I'm going to follow and all the things I'll do tomorrow. My search for satori changes subtly. And one day I know I *have* changed. Something has happened to me that I don't understand. But I understand Jack. And I understand Harry. And I laugh bitterly. Some days I wonder how it happened, but there's always a bottle to console me. And how does it happen? I don't know? Maybe born with a thirst unquenchable? Maybe I was greedy? Or lazy when I found I could get my adventure easy in a shiny barroom? No need to go into the cold and the wind and the rain when I can dream in a drink. Day after day I come out of the shop with a bottle in a bag in a tight grip and walk past the drunks on the benches and shake my head at their sorrow. Then one day I can't wait. So I sit on the bench and take a drink and watch a young man—just like I once was—with a bottle in a paper bag walking past the drunks, and he watches me and shakes his head. And I rub my chin, and it occurs to me that I can't remember how long since I shaved.

But on that morning of my youth, with stubble on my chin and Harry sleeping, the bench of drunken men is a long ways off. And that Atlantic beach further still. My thought that morning was that it was time to get going. I was done, ready to go. I'd walk as long as necessary to catch a ride or find a crossroad or something. Harry could have his homemade wine and his drunk farm. I'd wait for him to wake, then tell him and be gone. He could follow or not, his choice.

I left the old man sleeping and walked out to the lake. The moisture in the air gave the world a shimmer. A bird cried loudly, but remained unseen. This day bright, green pines, still lake, a slight, damp chill, not uncomfortable, beautiful.

Huckleberry Hound lay curled by the door of the boathouse. He lifted his head to greet me with a soft growl. Offshore, the last whiskey bottle floated neck-up. Its lip held the sun, casting a translucent shadow on the water. I recall the calmness of it all, like some elaborate deadfalls trap, not quite hidden, waiting to drop at the slightest disruption of its trigger.

It was time for me to go.

But do I really remember the foreboding? Did I wake feeling the breath of fate? I don't know. I can only do my best to reconstruct the events as I remember them. That's the problem with trying truly to recall the emotions of the past—you know what happens next.

I kneeled in the sand and performed my morning ablutions, then relit the fire. I filled the kettle and put it to boil in the flame resurrected. I walked over toward the boathouse to get some coffee and find something to eat, expecting Huckleberry to skedaddle as he and the others had done before. But something had changed. He didn't move until I was pretty close and then only to stand and raise his hair and snarl. I backed off and picked up a chunk of wood, a hefty bit of log that was half-charred, and threw it. Not to hit the dog, but hard against the side of the building to make a loud noise and show I meant business. The hound got the message and skedaddled.

The back room was a wreck. We'd left the door open the night before. Ration boxes were torn and scattered. The dogs? Most likely. Or maybe? I smiled, Harry looking for booze after I'd gone to sleep. What wasn't a can was ripped open. Must have been quite a party. No wonder Huckleberry was in such a foul mood. If I had eaten that combination I'd be cranky too. The coffee was safe in a can. Most of the cigarettes were torn up, but not completely. I found a few whole ones, grabbed a tin, *Chopped Ham and Eggs*, glad the pooches hadn't figured out how to open cans.

Smoke from my cigarette swirled with steam from the coffee. I had time to think. I'd managed to outrun my life for a few days, but this pastoral gave it leave to catch me. I should be graduating in a couple of months. I had no course for the future. I wondered if Huckleberry was happy living here in the forest. Did he miss the warm kitchen fire and the twice-daily bowl of kibble? Were the hard times, hungry days and cold nights, and the ticks and the fleas, the awful thunderstorms worth the exaltation of a raw, primitive survival? I didn't know, had no answer. So I sat and smoked and waited for the drunk I was to become to awaken.

Harry blinked, blinded by the day. He shielded his eyes with his hand, looked across the camp. "Shit. Shit. Shit. And a good God damn." He walked out past the firepit. "Coffee?" I asked. He waved me off and went toward the lake, paused at the fifty gallons of fermentation, gave it a pat, then got down carefully in the sand. He splashed water on his face, and again, took some in his cupped hands to drink. He then retched horribly, his body shaking with spasms over and over until his gut was empty and then some. "Sonofabitch."

I didn't say anything, simply watched. It took some time. He squinted at the lake. Pushed himself up to stand. Stood unsteadily and began to walk into the water. No shoes, but pants, shirt, as if he were walking on dry land, his eyes fixed ahead. I had no idea. Had he gone mad? Was he drowning himself? Maybe he wanted to cool off? The bottom was sand and shallow, and he was only thigh deep when he reached the bottle, sun still glinting off its neck. He picked it up and looked through it and held it to his lips to drain whatever was in it.

He spit out.

"JesusMaryJoseph."

He flung the bottle out into the lake. "Man overboard," said softly. He turned, temporarily defeated, walked back to me. All he'd gotten was lake water.

"Starting. Starting that bad feeling," he said to me. "Starting them DTs."

"Me too." I arrogantly thought I was feeling a bit of the DTs myself, as if my sick stomach and headache and gentle longing for some hair-of-the-dog was anything like what Harry was beginning to feel.

Harry held his arm out straight, his hand palm down with fingers together. He hadn't had any booze since the evening before. He slowly spread his fingers, and as they spread they began to shake. And the shaking fingers took over the hand, and the hand shook, and the shaking moved up his arm till he snatched it back. I held my hand out too. It was also shaking, but not like Harry's. "It's that G.I. coffee," I said. "They made it strong in those days."

Harry took a deep breath. Inspiration. Expiration. Aspiration. "Okay now. We just gotta pull ol' Harry together. Done it before. Done it again. Done, done endure.

"Insides all's a quivering. Wait it out. Sweat it out."

That's how it starts.

"Worst part ... worst part's knowing what's coming next." He looked into my eyes for something I could not give him. "Ya know what's coming?" I didn't, not at all, not yet.

The "bad-feeling" he called it—a special kind of extreme discomfort. "Insides all's a quivering," is a good description. It feels like all your internal organs are vibrating gently and quietly. It's not the shaking hand, not that outward, visible shaking—you get that too. But this internal quivering is somehow worse. It wears on you. It's the buzzing of a light when you're trying to read quietly. Think of the hum of a fluorescent lamp that's going bad. Imagine putting your hand on it, feel the way it's humming. Keep your hand on it. Don't move your hand. Try to forget the humming. You can almost ignore it if you find something to distract you, but once you start to think about it, and to feel it, you can't get rid of it. Take your hand away, it stays with you. Once you let it in it will consume you. That's how it feels. Except it's inside of you. It's not some lamp's transformer going bad. It's your insides going bad, and you can't flick the switch or unplug it or move away from it, because wherever you go, whatever you do, it goes with you and vibrates inside of you. And sometimes it feels so deep inside that you think it's not physical at all, that it's in your soul. And whether you stand or sit or walk or run or jump up and jump down or lie curled up in a fetal position, you can't escape it. But you know how to make it go away. There's only one way.

"I guess we's out?"

"Yes."

"That bottle you brung out last night?" His voice trailed off in resignation. "Ain't no more?" He knew already.

"Coffee?" Harry sat across from me and nodded, offered the cup, pulled it back for me to stop halfway, held it in two hands, raised it to his lips with a jerk to drink.

He looked up at me and smiled weakly, shook his head.

"Sometimes I just want it to stop. Stop so I can catch a breath. Only a minute's. All's I's asking."

"It's stopped now," I said. "Here, on the lake, you can stop and rest."

"No son," he said sweetly. "Jus' starting. It's just starting up."

An experienced drinker, a serious drinker, someone who drinks and stays drunk for weeks and weeks, months and months, years and years, and has a full-blown dependence on alcohol, knows what's coming next. Harry knew what was coming for him. I had no idea. DTs, delirium tremens, Harry explained as best he could, when you stop your drinking your body goes through withdrawal. I heard about heroin withdrawal, but not from booze. You have to drink long and hard to saturate your body to create the kind of dependence that leads to the delirium tremens. It's, like it says, *delirium* and *tremors*. It's why Harry was shaking so much. It was also why he sweated and shivered simultaneously. And the delirium? We were driving down that road.

"What's that damn dog doing?"

The doberman was watching us from the door of the boathouse. "Cerberus. Guarding the gate of Hades! Is ya?" Harry grabbed a log and threw it at the dog. He missed, and Cerberus skedaddled. "Damn dogs.

"Ain't going to no Hades! Ain't going in no box! Harry's tougher than any damn dog."

We hadn't seen much of the dogs during the day. Prior, they had made their presence known at dusk and during the night by roaming the margins of the woods. But they were getting bolder, getting used to us. We had food and had been feeding them, and they had been taking the scraps. The previous night's party had no doubt given them ideas of entitlement. The doberman was back on the edge of the trees watching. Harry's log throwing wasn't enough to chase him for long, and he'd picked up his faithful companion Rin Tin Tin. Emboldened perhaps by his bigger companions, Scruffy Terror came across the yard, snarled at us in passing and lifted his leg to pee on our winemaking project. Harry hefted another log but held back, fearful I suppose of disturbing the fermentation. I was more concerned with the puppies. They were young and fearless, and if they came up to us the others might try to protect them. Making friends with feral dogs, that might have been a mistake.

Harry sipped coffee and struggled to hold it in his stomach. He sat up some and took another sip, then slid down till his back rested on the sand, his head propped up by the log.

"I'm gonna lie down a bit." He rolled on his side to push himself up. "Sleep it off. Got to endure." The way he stumbled it took him some effort to get to the cabin. He stood at the door and looked back. "Not gonna be wandering off and getting lost again? No? Don't wanna be having to find ya all over again."

I wanted to tell him that I was going, that I'd had enough.

"I'll be here," I said. "I'll be fine. I won't wander off."

Poor sot, as if he were the one taking care of me.

A crash from the cabin told me he had stumbled. I listened. He picked himself up, crashed again, then quiet. "Now's my chance," I thought. "Time to go." It was a pleasant day. Not too hot, not too cold, the sun had burned off the shimmer. There was a crystalline clarity to the air. A few insects were flying about. A breeze rippled the water. A fish broke the surface. It was a perfect day to walk out.

No, I wouldn't leave him. The trigger had tripped. I was trapped. I shook my head in resignation. The Christian girl had said, "Having a conscience proves you have a soul." I wondered, "Did I?" A week ago there had been no old Harry. I had been slogging my way up Wisconsin 51, getting short, friendly rides from locals. The Christian girl drove an hour each way to spend her nights cleaning stainless steel vats in a cheese-puff factory. "I climb right in and scrub 'em. They like me 'coz I'm small and get in the hatches." It was a good ride and gave me a chance to get warm. She asked if I was ok, offered to buy me breakfast, but I wanted to keep moving, didn't want to risk a conversion. I didn't exactly argue with her, but I didn't agree either. She gave me five bucks and her heartfelt prayer. "Jesus be with you. You ask Him."

Soul or no soul, I'd wait a day. I couldn't leave him any more than I could burst that poor girl's bubble and tell her that there was no God. Harry and I would walk out together. We were a team, right? Let him sleep. Time for old Harry to sober up. Then get the hell out.

Listless, I watched the lake. I picked my scab till it bled. Smoked my last good smokes. Noticed as small, dark bumps rose oddly on the surface of the water. They came up slowly—then zip. Gone in an instant. It took some time, and not a few occasions of their appearance (and disappearance) for me to even believe that they were indeed real. It took some more time to realize that they were turtles poking up their heads. They were very cautious, and after a while, I would remain very still as they rose, then make them disappear with a snap of my fingers. That's what it had come to, my Romance of the road, waiting for the old, drunken Harry to sober up and troubling turtles through the afternoon. Well, even Jack had his slow days.

Late, late afternoon, a muffled crash announced that Harry was awake. There was a fair amount of banging, and I had almost gotten up to see what was happening when he tumbled down the steps, barely not falling, grabbing the first sapling for support. He had an idea—the only idea that could have rousted him from his slumbers. "I've been studying on it." Harry pointed to his head so I would know that he had been studying.

"This gentleman. Gentleman who constructed this paradise. I'm speculating. He was, well maybe he's not who constructed this, maybe he didn't, maybe he was visiting. Maybe renting for the season. Gentleman who lived here, he was a sporting man. Man who lived here liked to drink." Said softly and carefully so as not to break the spell he had cast.

"We got to search. Before we lose the light. Light go out. Out go the light, and we got no 'lectricy." He pointed to sun. "See here, that bottle you got back that rubbish. Man hid that there. Bottle I found in the boot. Man hid that too. All them bottles in the trash. Man was more than just a drinker. Serious about his drinking he was. Serious drinkers don't run out. Stash some for a rainy day. Rainy day come and gone. Man done gone." It was Harry that was gone. He was giddy, excited, shaking from withdrawal. No doubt feeling pretty bad now. He'd figured out a prospect for getting some booze. "We got to look. Ain't got no flashlight. Got no flashlight, do ya?

"Just asking Ya for one more bottle. Just a pint. Just asking for a pint to get to when the wine's ready. Ready in a day or two. Just a pint, fifth be good too. Nurse it. Sip here and there. Keep her going till the big batch is done." He was laying out his deal with God. "After that. I'll be good. Get this ol' drunk farm going. Helping Ya out Lord. Helping Ya out. You and me, saving them souls."

I remembered he'd said the same thing when I brought out the bottle from behind the boathouse, that he'd nurse it. It would last for the next couple of days, till the fruit had fermented and turned into wine. But that bottle had only lasted couple of hours. The last thing I wanted was for him to continue until the wine fermented. We'd be here for a week. No, he had to get right so I could take him out with me. I had half a mind to dump out the wine and get it over with. I was just a kid. I didn't know what to do. It was beyond my experience. Literature was no help at all. (I didn't understand DTs. I hadn't read Kerouac's *Big Sur* yet. It sat on my shelf, spine unbroken. I would read it someday along with *Satori in Paris* and shudder.) All I knew was that I couldn't leave him like he was. When he was feeling better, it would be his choice. I'd give him the choice (As if he had any choice. God help me, I didn't know.) to stay and wait for the wine or walk out with me. Harry went from tree to tree, gripping each to keep from falling. When he stopped, his left leg shook uncontrollably. The shaking came in spasms, between them he moved to the next tree.

"Ya got's to help me look. We's a team, share and share alike. I shared my bottle with ya. Shared it right? Shared my bottle?"

He saw me watching.

He said, "Ya gotta out think 'em. Got to think like a drunk."

"Shouldn't be a problem," I replied.

"Thought you was my friend?"

"Sorry."

"Why you got to be so mean?"

"Sorry."

He knew he was a drunk, and often referred to himself as a drunk or some such signifier, but he didn't really accept it, didn't really believe it. I didn't understand it at the time, but the beatest stumblebum will take offense when someone else calls them a drunk—until the moment they admit it to themselves.

But at that moment Harry was a belligerent, old boozer stuck in denial, stuck in the woods, stuck with no booze, and delirium tremens his immediate future. Unless ...

"We gotta find it boy. You gonna help or not?"

I nodded yes. I'd help him. We were a team. I wondered to myself what the hell I was going to do. I should have shouldered my pack and walked out. Walking out all the way the Atlantic if I didn't get a ride. I felt sorry for him. Maybe we'd find a pint, then I could convince him to walk out with me.

Thus the hunt for the booze began.

"Been looking in the cabin," he explained. He had a plan. "You look there. Look there case I missed something. Two eyes is better 'en one."

Harry had indeed searched the cabin. Everything was flung down and strewn about, including the contents of my rucksack. He'd been pretty desperate to throw caution to the wind and mess with my stuff again. I didn't know where to begin. Where does one hide the booze? Why does one hide the booze? I pushed around cans and jars that were still in the cupboards. But we'd been through it with the dusty cordials. I felt in the low spaces under the counter. It seemed futile. Harry had looked. He was the professional boozer. He'd know where to look. I looked around the bunk beds and sat down, looked under the mattresses and suddenly had a brainstorm. Animated by the hunt, I looked under the boards that supported the mattresses. There was a space under there! I was excited about finding a bottle, but discovered only a nest of paper and rags and acorn shells. Disappointed and a bit ashamed, we didn't even know if another bottle existed. What was I getting excited about?

The old man was shouting something, calling for me to help. He wasn't in the boathouse. I heard his voice around back, off in the woods. I followed a rut, well-worn but overgrown. He was trying to lift what was once a wall of the outhouse. The old shitter had long ago tumbled to the ground, fallen over and collapsed onto itself at the same time, as if a giant hand had pushed it down and over. Harry was struggling with one of the walls, but it was covered with roof. It was clear that we'd be better off to remove what was on it first, which is what I started doing. Harry kept lifting, waiting for the moment that he could move the wall and uncover the long unused hole.

"Toilet tank," he said mysteriously. "Where the water is, drunks always hide their booze in the tank. In ya go and get a drink. Nice and private. Keeps it cool too. Nobody knows it's there."

"Except all the drunks," I said. And avoided the obvious comment that the outhouse didn't have toilet, tank, water.

"I knows it ain't the same. But I'm thinking he stored his booze here too. Quick snort in the ol' head. Habits die hard."

I got the debris cleared off and moved over to help Harry with the wall. We lifted the edge and tossed it to the side. Harry looked expectantly into the hole. I got the impression that he was thinking his bottle of booze would magically shimmer and light up, glow like some pot of coins or golden treasure in a cartoon. It was just a black pit. What had been the seat and the floor were collapsed and rotten, and Harry, on his knees at the edge, tore at them to open up the hole. We still couldn't see much. Harry was down on his belly in a flash, reaching down into the pit with his hands, sliding forward to get deeper. "Damn, hold me so's I don't fall in this sonofabitch."

Mercifully, no one had used the facility for a long time. The effluence had dried up and turned into whatever old shit turns into. "Got it!

"Pull me back."

I did, and he got his prize clear of the edge. It was just the neck and top half. The bottom was broken. "See. Getting close," Harry said in triumph.

He kept leaning in with two hands digging. I held with all my strength to keep him from disappearing. "Ouch! Sonofabitch!" And he kept on and on until it was more than clear that there wasn't a bottle down there.

"Harry," I pleaded. "It's not there. It's getting dark. We need to look in other places." I didn't mind looking, but not there. "The guy had a whole woods to hide it in. He wouldn't put it down with a pile of fresh shit."

My logic must have impressed him. "Get me out," he said. I pulled him up. When he pushed off the edge of the hole his hands were filthy, but I could see the dark red seeping out.

"Harry! You're bleeding." There might be a worse place than the business end of an old shitter to slice open your hand, but I couldn't think of one. "We need to clean that up. We need to wash it, put something on it."

"Naw. It's fine. We gotta look."

Blood was dripping down his arm. He'd really opened up his finger. I had a handkerchief in my back pocket. I gave it to him to wrap around, soak up the blood, if not stop it.

"Plenty of time later," he said as he wrapped his wound. He was shaking badly. The handkerchief kept unwrapping. He had to hold it with his good hand. We needed some tape, or bandage, or string to hold it on. "Let's look in the boathouse," I suggested to get him away from the outhouse.

Harry agreed. I figured there'd be something. I vaguely remembered a first aid kit.

The sun was low enough to be making shafts through the busted wall. The bottles that Harry and I had pulled from the trash drum were still lined up on the workbench, illuminated as if some mocking God wanted to highlight Harry's struggle--just like a cartoon. I'd forgotten all about them. To me they were empty, but Harry was a pro. He found a mayonnaise jar that held nails, dumped the nails, set it on the bench, and upended the first bottle, all set to drip. I spun around the room with my eyes and stopped on the first aid kit. The gentleman may or may not have been a bottle-hiding drunk, but he was savvy enough to put a first aid kit in a prominent place so anyone could find it in a hurry.

The floor was littered with bottles we'd dumped to get at the fifty gallon drum for the fermentation project. Many of the bottles had corks in them and still held a few drops of the precious elixir. Harry collected them, looked at each carefully, put the promising ones on the workbench. I popped the first aid kit open and fished out a bottle of iodine and some bandages. "Harry! Leave it for a minute. We've got to wash and bandage you up." He ignored me. "Fine." I put the stuff down and grabbed a bucket and filled it with water from the lake, then made Harry stick his hand in it and swirl it around. I poured on some iodine and wrapped a clean bandage around the still bleeding finger. It was all I could do. Harry sniffed the air, suddenly intrigued, took the iodine and smelled it, then drank what was left.

Tincture of iodine, alcohol, but not for drinking. He fought to hold it down, but it came right back up. With his mouth and lips and chin stained with the red and the madness in his eyes he looked ... well you can imagine.

The tincture made him all the more desperate. The mayonnaise jar project was slowly paying out. "Always a drop or two left," he told me. There was a slim quarter-inch in the bottom, a swallow almost. And it made his day, this little tease of nectar.

"Look. Look," he said to me. "Out back where you found the other one, before the light goes."

The building and trees put the rubbish in deep shadow. I had to be careful walking on the rusted junk. I moved things and peered into crevices. I double-checked where I had found the other bottle. I was catching the old man's desperation and had to fight it off. "I could use a drink right now," I thought, perhaps even said aloud. I kept looking, overturning what I could. Maybe it was at the bottom? Maybe he had hidden one and forgotten it, and it had been covered up? Should I get a shovel? Digging with my hands I realized all the glass. I needed some gloves. Even as I searched I understood the futility of it all, looking for a bottle in a pile of long discarded rubbish. But I went on. It was too late in the day to walk out. A nice bottle of Scotch would be wonderful. We would have a fine evening. I would make a mulligan. Not drink too much —a drink or three to take the edge off. I would tell Harry I was leaving the next day. He would make his own choice as to what to do. We'd have a fine time. Where was that bottle?

"You look in the ceiling? In the cabin." Harry had an idea.

"No," I answered and moved toward his voice in the boathouse.

"Sonofabitch. I forgot. There's a hatch in there. Up in that ceiling. You look?"

I hadn't and said so and crossed carefully over the rubbish and around the corner of the boathouse in time to see Harry lunging across the yard. Rin Tin Tin had been snooping around. Harry's shouting and bursting out of the boathouse so sudden spooked the pooch. And it responded as a frightened dog will. Rin was on Harry in a second. It was good that Harry had baggy pants, because from what I could see, that's most of what Rin got of him. I'd left the ill-fated fish spear leaning against the side of the boathouse and instinctively grabbed it and cocked my arm back to throw. I hesitated. I didn't want to kill. I didn't want to go through all that stabbing again. The fish's death saved that poor pooch. I turned the spear and stepped forward with the butt end. Harry was crawling on the ground, and Rin Tin Tin was trying for a better grip when I caught Rin on the flank with the shaft. That didn't quite get his attention, so I whacked him again on the side of the head. The dog turned on me, and as I swung a third time he had the end of the spear in his jaws.

Harry crawled to the cabin.

I shouted.

"DOWN.

"DROP IT!"

And damn if something long-remembered in that dog didn't kick in, and he opened his mouth and sat down pretty as you please. I was sorry I didn't have a treat for him. After a few seconds, he offered me his paw. No hard feelings. I had sense enough not to take the paw or pet him or do anything, but backed away very slowly toward the cabin.

I kept the spear ahead of me and closed the door as best it could close. Harry used the table to pull himself up and sit. His hands and legs were shaking, really shaking, shaking like I had never seen before and couldn't believe. He started to rise, but shook so much that he fell back into his seat.

"I gotta get some."

I thought the shaking was from fear, exertion from the dog. That was part of it, but mostly it was the booze. I didn't realize what not having a drink could do to a person. Harry needed a drink. "Look," he said and pointed. "Up there."

There was a ceiling, and there was the hatch in the middle. I hadn't noticed before. I pulled up a chair and used it to get on the table and then pulled it up on the table so I could get up and stick my head well into the hatch. Harry was in no condition to do anything. I pushed the hatch up and out of the way and stuck my head and shoulders up in the dead space. It looked empty, just rafters and some kind of loose flocking for insulation, hardly enough room even to crawl into. And except for the bit of light from the hatch, very dark.

"Nothing. I can't see it's so dark."

"Look good, son. Got to be there."

I pulled myself up into the hatch with a little jump and lay on my stomach and felt around as best I could. I dug my hands into the ancient insulation. Whatever was up there I figured would be close to the edge. "Nothing," I called to Harry.

"It's up there." Harry, in his desperation, had convinced himself that a bottle was hidden somewhere. I was almost convinced myself, as if we were on a treasure hunt, that someone had indeed hidden a bottle for us. It was the golden Easter egg, and we just had to find it. I sifted the insulation with my hands. Nothing. "It's not here Harry."

"No. No. What was I thinking?" he said. "Weren't no drunk putting no booze up there. Too hard to git at."

Relieved that Harry given up on the hatch and rafters, I slipped back and dropped onto the table.

Crash!

I hit the chair hard and sideways and knocked it over and Harry fell off his chair and let out a yelp. I was on my ass on the floor, the chair overturned, the table askew. Well, no harm done. Harry was getting on my nerves. I was getting careless.

"What's this? This here. Here look!" said Harry sprawled on the floor. "I'll be damned and delivered."

"What?" I was on the floor, ready to tell Harry that I was done with his stupid search.

Our falls had knocked aside a thin mat that had been on the floor under the table. There was a trapdoor under the mat. Harry was on his knees pushing the mat aside and tugging the door open, another dark hole of vain hope. Harry put his head in and then a little farther. "God damn. Get me a light." And then he fell in, just his legs sticking out. It was only about two feet.

"Christ. I can't see nothing."

Then a commotion, Harry's legs kicking. "JesusMary! Get me out! They're attacking!"

Harry had found the secret lair of the puppies. I pulled him up. His nose was bleeding. Not a nosebleed, but blood oozing out numerous, tiny punctures from tiny teeth. "Good thing momma wasn't down there," I laughed.

"Damn dogs.

"Git me a light." He wasn't done yet.

I had the lantern. I didn't trust Harry with it. I was ready to leave, but not fleeing a fire. I said I'd do it. I lit the lantern and lowered my head into the hole with the puppies. The lantern scared them into a corner. There was a pit, lined with wood, directly below the hatch. The pups had a nice nest, but no booze.

A shaft of gray light in the corner behind the pups showed where they came and went. Then the light was blocked, and a growl told me it was time to pull my head up. Momma dog, or maybe uncle Rin Tin Tin, was headed my way. I pulled myself and the light out of the hole and dropped the door as the big dog switched from growl to bark.

Harry rubbed his nose.

"See anything?"

"No."

He, or I, could have really gotten torn up. What would I do? It was odd to feel so cut off. A broken leg, a bad dog-bite, I had thought of myself as so free and independent and self-sufficient on the road. But I wasn't. On the highway I was still cradled in civilization, the land of friendly strangers and handouts. And hospitals if I got hurt or sick, restrooms, running water, hamburgers, cold beer.

"We got them bottles in the boathouse." In his excitement about the hatch, he'd left the upside down bottle project, but just for a moment. "Got me some."

"The dogs," I reminded him.

In the yard the dogs were circling. Twilight, it was their time and the first time I'd seen what I supposed was the whole pack out of the underbrush—Cerberus and Rin Tin Tin, who stood out as leaders, Huckleberry, Snow White and her seven puppies, the Shaggy Terror. And besides the ones we had named, there were half-dozen or more creatures of uncertain identity. I remember one with a limp, old, gray, sad. They kept moving in and out of the trees. I didn't know what they wanted. Dogs, who knows what they really are thinking? It's hard enough with people, and we have language and are at least of the same species. Luckily, in this case, I knew what Harry wanted and he, Harry, had an idea of what the dogs wanted.

"They want to eat us," he said. "But ol' Harry's smarter than any damn dog."

I wasn't so sure. He was on the floor. His mouth stained still with the iodine, his hair wild, his yesterday-new clothing filthy, feral eyes of desperation —all combined to give him a singular appearance. Except for the mouth, and maybe the eyes, I probably didn't look much better. We were animals ourselves. But we could open cans. And we did.

I don't know if it was comic or tragic. The modes swirl and interweave, and I am never sure how to judge these events. In the end, the distinction seems artificial. So for now, call it comedy as we opened cans of ration gruel and dumped sludge into pots and made balls and threw them into the woods.

I wonder sometimes the connections that dogs make—do they have an idea of cause and effect? Do they carry magical thinking? Did the circling bring them the manna from cabin? Did some prayer on their part bring balls of meat flung into the woods? Did Rin Tin Tin think that his trick of sitting was the cause of this windfall? Did each dog have his or her own idea of a cause? Or did they make no connection at all? Their actions and this gift of this food—no connection. It was just what happened, like the rain or the sun or the fall of a pinecone or the dash of a rabbit across a clearing.

They probably weren't as philosophic about it as I was. They ate it up, and we took our pots and moved across the yard tossing morsels into the woods and making a path for ourselves to the golden elixir. Harry couldn't stand it and made a lunge for the boathouse door. "No," I shouted. "Don't run!" An anonymous, shaggy beast, a youngster with a black back and light brown underside, went after him. Chase instinct kicking in. Harry held his pot of glop over his head as if he didn't want the dog to get it. The human-selfish instinct, or the Harry-selfish instinct, kicking in. "Give him the pot." Harry misunderstood my words and swung the pot at the dog's head. He missed. If it had been a person they would have exacted their revenge by mauling Harry, but the pooch only ducked away to grab the gruel that had slopped out when Harry took his swing. I slowly eased past the gorging dog, dumping my load next to its head. The pooch growled at me, but kept on with eating.

"See if ya can find some rat poison," Harry ordered me. "Gonna feed them dogs right." And he turned to work on his draining project.

There was no way I was going to kill the dogs. But I was concerned that they would follow the food into the boathouse. I shifted some of the wooden crates from the backroom to make a barrier across the door. My backwoods bartender did his darnedest to get every last drop out of those bottles. He took his time now. The anticipation was profound. He truly believed that this next round would set his world right.

I don't know how long. I was exhausted and sat. "I need some light." I lit a match. Harry looked at the tease of booze in the mayonnaise jar. He smelled it and smiled. "Blended. I prefer the single malts, but we can't be choosey, can we?" He was trying to be cool, to save face and not let on how desperate he was for the drink. He shook so that I was afraid he would upset the whole thing. I could see it took all he had to sip it slowly. Then he tilted his head back and poured it in straight, holding the jar with two hands and thrusting it against his mouth to brace so the shaking didn't spill it out. The look on his face told me that it didn't go down smoothly. Another match. He looked right at me —handsome and tragic, flickering flame masking the pain and scars of his life. Gulping it had been a mistake. My heart went out to him. He needed that booze in his blood. I was afraid he'd puke it up and lose it. He almost did, holding the jar under his mouth to catch that which might come up.

At last let he out a great smiling burp, and we were both pleased.

Barring the tincture of iodine, it was the first alcohol in him since the night before. It invigorated him as it made him desperate for more. "Jesus, I gotta get some in me," he pleaded to the universe. "Just gotta."

I couldn't help him.

"Gotta. Wine's ready? Maybe? How many days it's been?"

"Two."

"Two full days?"

"No, not till tomorrow morning. Day before yesterday we set it up."

"Damn. Damn drinker. What'd he do with his booze? Gotta be more. Tip of the iceberg. Iceberg got a tip. All's we finding is iceberg's tip. Sonofabitch. What do ya do?"

His eyes lit up. This drunken genius grabbed an empty whiskey bottle and headed for the door. He scrambled over my barrier of ration boxes to fall headfirst. Stopped, quiet now. He'd killed himself, knocked himself senseless? Out cold? No, he had remembered, stopped and listened. He got up slowly. God only knows where the pooches went off to. To the doggie clinic to have their stomachs pumped? Harry held the bottle as a club and proceeded with caution to the cabin. He went in, and I followed, cautious about the dogs. He set the flipped table back upright and righted the chair to sit in. He put the bottle down on the table and lifted a glass to his lips. But he didn't have a glass in his hand. He tossed back whatever imaginary liquid was in the imaginary glass. Whiskey I supposed. He'd gone mad. Did that help? Could he pretend to drink and get drunk? Kerouac said that the world is an illusion. Was Jack right? Could Harry make the illusion of the world work itself into a bottle of booze?

No, Harry had a more practical idea. After he'd finished the glass. "Ready about." He stood and took the bottle to the doorway. "Hard a-lee." And flung it into the underbrush. "Man overboard.

"There," he said to me and pointed to where the bottle had landed. "That's the sweet spot. Sweet spot where he tossed the empties. Sporting man like myself gets the urge sometimes to quit. Quit it. Quit before the bottle's empty. Quit before the bottle quits him. Corks 'er up. Out she goes. Bombs away. Just gotta find her now."

I had to admit, it made sense. I guess my idea of what made sense, what constituted rational thought and the power it held to explain reality, was rapidly deteriorating. His little play-acting made perfect sense to me at the time. And I was looking forward to the drink myself.

So we scrambled in the underbrush on our insane Easter egg hunt, hunting the golden egg. It was after all, spring. Why not? Maybe it was Easter? Maybe it was Sunday? I hadn't been keeping track. Harry got on his hands and knees feeling around. For myself, not quite willing to give up all pretense of dignity, I shuffled around feeling with my feet under the low plants and fallen needles for any bottles.

We didn't find anything at all. Not a dog poop to foul my shoe, not a rock to stub my toe, not a jagged edge for Harry to cut his finger on. It was hopeless, and we both knew it. After fifteen, maybe twenty minutes, long after it was apparent that our search was in vain, Harry stood up. He looked around as if he didn't want to go where he was going, just felt the need to go. He sighed and walked. Harry was headed to the wine. He walked slowly. I think he knew in his heart that his wine would be a bust. So much of Harry's life had been a bust. His mind was so addled by alcohol that whatever he did went wrong. And he knew it. It had happened so many times before, like winding up here in the pines. He should have walked out when he had booze still to sustain him. He knew that too. But it was too late. He figured it out long ago. He was a hopeless drunk, but there was a spark of something that kept him trying, perhaps the spark that is life— not a simple fire burning, but a glimpse of shadow in the shadows, a horn man's solo, a Wisconsin girl's faith, a bodhisattva who will set a drunk free.

So Harry walked to the fifty gallon drum of futility. He took the lid off and smelled. "Boy, git me that light." I saw the dogs over past the firepit in the shadow of the pines. We'd have to get the fire up. Cerberus had his nose in the air, and I could hear him snorting, trying to figure out what in Hell the humans were doing with that mad fermentation. I took the lantern over, and Harry snatched it away and peered into the mass of sugar and fruit cocktail. I was expecting more, some foul-smelling, bubbling broth of decay or something. But it was nothing, nothing seemed to have happened. It just smelled sweet like fruit cocktail. Nothing ... somehow that was the saddest thing.

"Can you get me m' mug?"

I did.

"I'm going to start the fire," I said.

The tinder was just taking hold as Harry sat down with a half full mug held in two hands, sweat rolling down his forehead. The tinder burst into a pyramid of fire. Everything inside of Harry was going wrong. "Got that bad feeling. Eh. What do ya do with a drunken sailor?" I had to give him credit. He was a tough, old coot. "Don't never be no drunk, son." A last bit of advice before stepping off the plank.

I don't think I've ever seen anything so full of the pity of humanity as Harry trying to not puke up his syrupy mix of forty-year-old army issue fruit cocktail and sugar. I could see it come up against his will and the full mouth of vomit that he forced down again. He burped. He sat and we waited. Waited and waited. Then he got up and went over to the drum. Hardly able to walk now, he seemed animated by some satanic force, arms and legs jerking in odd, purposeful spasms as he moved. He gained the drum and used the rim to steady himself and reached in and got another cup and drank it down, then took yet another and brought it back and sat on the log like some bhikku searching for satori, feeling his insides turning over and shaking and quivering, and in the sad upheaval that was his stomach trying to discover the soothing tranquilly that would come as the first hints of alcohol closed the gaps in his brain. He drank the third cup, sat and concentrated and kept himself from exploding from sheer force of will. I watched him with shame. It was like watching—what?—I don't know, a horrible scene in a play. But this wasn't a play.

This was a real person whose eyes glistened in the firelight and whose sweat-drenched shirt stuck to his distended stomach and who shivered and to whom

Truth came and sobbed and sobbed. "Damn. Damn. God damn sonofabitch." And he stood with a superhuman effort and ran and fell forward as he ran so he was falling and running toward the drum and knocked it over and fell on his knees. "Yeast. God damn. God damn. Ain't got no yeast. Got to put in the bread," he called to me. "Got to have yeast. Yeast to make it booze. It ain't nothing. We ain't got nothing. Nothing. No nothing. We got to get out of here. Got to go."

And he was up and off into the trees. Just like that. Of course, we needed yeast to get the fermentation going. I should have thought of that myself. But didn't. I didn't have any practical experience at homemade winemaking. Chemistry? I was an English major, what did I know? And for Harry, who did know, his mind was, well, fermented.

Tragic? Comic? I don't know? You decide.

I sat for a moment. It was like a play. Lear half-naked, half-mad wailing, railing against fate. But I wasn't watching a play. I wasn't audience. I was actor. I had to act. Not Lear, but my Harry in the night running to his doom. I expected the dogs to go for him. Maybe they did. I didn't see them. He was headed in the general direction of the road. I debated on taking the lantern. Decided I should. He'd see it and maybe find me. Harry would run into some tree and poke his eye out or stumble on some wind-fallen spike of a pine log. He'd kill himself. Trip and impale himself. And then what? What would I do? To be honest, I was as worried about myself as I was about Harry. Whatever happened to him, I would have to do something. Was he my responsibility? Not really. But that conscience, not my own, spoke to me. And what if he was just hurt? But hurt bad. What would I do? I should have just walked away two days ago. I should have just walked into the rain and thunder and left him to follow that damn cartoon arrow alone.

Funny how things work out.

I went to the dirt road we had followed in. It was overgrown, but still easier than bushwhacking as Harry seemed to be doing. I assumed that he would cut it and turn and follow it. I saw a single bright star. There was a gap, a canyon in the trees to let in the sky. Even with the lantern, I could follow the broken road more by looking up than down. I had to take care of the fallen trunks across my path. I heard some motion off to the right. It stopped when I did. I knew it was dogs. I needed to find Harry. I should have brought the canteen. Maybe he needed some water? Ahead, up the road but out of my vision, I heard a commotion.

Over the past days I'd let myself believe that we were isolated, miles from anywhere or anyone, alone in our own wilderness. Yet all the while we'd been fairly close to a spot where the local kids partied. Off to the side of the trash pile, which blocked our road and protected our privacy, was a couch and couple of chairs arranged around a firepit. That was where I found Harry. He was picking up empties and shaking them, smelling them, taking a sip here and again, spitting out or swallowing depending what he found. I watched him spit out a cigarette butt without blink or pause. The big rain of the other night had put water into the empties and diluted whatever beer was left. But not every local finished their beer, and Harry got a few watery mouthfuls. He was on his hands and knees, demanding the lantern light here and there. He found an empty pint of something, vodka perhaps, and held it up to his lips for a long time to drain the last drops. He clamored over a pile of ancient construction material that had been almost reduced to dirt—plaster and lath, it must have been some time ago, covered with vines and sprouting three small pines. "Watch out for snakes," I called as he pulled up an old hollow-core door, which bent and ripped and delaminated in his hands.

"Snakes," I remember saying. I wanted to say something, to use language to reaffirm my humanity while surrounded by feral dogs and pines and Harry. Harry was more out of control than any human I could believe. I tried to help, walking around with the lantern, Harry simply crawling and grunting and pointing where he wanted light. I was standing, and he was on his knees. He turned his head up to me, a streak of dirt where he'd brushed his hand across his forehead, sweating face, quivering lips—stained still red—hands clawing blindly for more, eyes terror, humanity gone.

There were trash bags and cases of empties and pizza boxes and bags from fast food torn asunder. Harry looked into heavy cardboard beer cases and peered through each bottle, holding it between his vision and the lantern. When he found some residue he just drank it. With a few, with their lids closed, the rain hadn't gotten in. He flipped the next case open and fell back as if he'd been hit. "JesusMary. Mother of God." He pulled out a bottle with the cap on, "I'll be damned and delivered."

It was empty. Someone had simply finished and pushed the cap back on. He was crushed. He fell back on his haunches and to the ground on his butt. Not anger, defeat. But there was another one with the cap on. I pulled it out. This was full. A forgotten soldier. I showed it to Harry.

He tried to twist off the cap, but it wasn't that kind. Now what? He smashed the neck against some wood, nothing doing. His eye caught the abandoned toilet. He got up, not without some trouble, fell, rolled to his knees and crawled the ten feet to it. He smashed the neck off and poured beer down his throat. He was renewed, his hope restored. He kept searching. I got sick of looking and sat on a Naugahyde chair. I wondered if it was Saturday, or Friday night. I had lost track and was too tired to figure it out. How many days, three, two, one thousand? It seemed like a long while, and it seemed like the flash of a moment. Maybe the locals would show up. What the hell would I tell them? I was ready to leave. Maybe in the morning we could go?

All has its limit—even the night sky stops somewhere. Harry's energy and desperation and hope had their's. He sat in the Naugahyde chair across from me.

"Time to go home, Harry."

"Home?"

"Back to the cabin."

He was dirty and stinking from crawling around garbage, wet and moldy and rotten Harry mixed with shit and urine. I stood to leave, and he reached out to me, held his hand out for me to take. And I hesitated. I didn't want to touch him. He saw it. And I saw that he saw it. This stays with me. And I am sorry to this day —"I'm sorry Harry."

It was as if some divine joker had wanted to push us both to the point where our humanity ceased. Then satisfied, let us go on with the knowledge of what we had so easily become.

I took his hand and pulled him up. He couldn't walk unaided. His legs began to quiver and quiver, and he leaned heavily against me until the shaking slowed down and he could get hold of himself.

"Come back tomorrow. Look good." He never gave up.

It surprised me how dark the world under the pines had become.

With Harry's arm on my shoulder, my arm around his waist, the lantern light dancing on the trees and the sandy road, we made our way back to camp.

The fire was quietly burning. I sat Harry on a log, and he slid himself down to the sand while I added wood to bring up the flame. The pine flared fast. I was still a bit worried about the dogs. I believed that the flames kept them back. I took the lantern into the boathouse to find some food. I'd make a big stew.

"Maybe it woulda turned out."

"Turned out what?"

"The wine. Maybe it woulda turned out ok. Maybe I shouldn't dumped it out?"

"I don't know. You said it needed yeast."

"Used to put bread in, when ya couldn't get yeast. Maybe if we got bread?"

"If we could get bread, we could get booze," I pointed out.

"College boy," said sweetly. "You're a good boy."

I walked over to the fallen drum. There were dog prints and scrapes from paws. They'd been eating, a dog feast.

"Do you want something to eat?"

"Not right now, thank you." I supposed that single beer had taken the edge off for a moment.

I boiled my mulligan. I hadn't eaten and was hungry. Mixed with the smoke from the pine, it smelled better than it would taste. I waited, enjoying the fiction of anticipation. Harry excused himself. His legs were shaking. He could barely stand. When he tried to move forward he fell down. "Guess my legs done gone to sleep. Sleepy old legs. Getting tired," said with a weak smile. As before, he groped from tree to tree, then gave up and crawled into the darkness. He stunk, the butt of his pants was stained brown. Should I try to help him clean himself up? I didn't want to. In the morning we'd have to get him into some clean clothes, plenty in the cabin. We'd never get a ride with him like this. I heard him crash down. Poor Harry. I didn't get up to help. He could keep whatever dignity he had left. He did something in the trees, peed, shit himself, made some groaning noises, crawled back to the fire and curled himself on the sand.

I didn't disturb him, had a cup of the stew and leaned back to look at the stars, moved away from the fire, away from its light so I could better see the night.

I dozed.

The stewpot falling woke me. The fire was down to embers. The dogs were stalking my mulligan. One must have gotten to it and knocked it over and then been scared back. I lay still in the dark. They were circling us, cautious. I watched Harry. He was either sleeping or ignoring the action, too miserable to care about what was happening around him. I hadn't startled awake, hadn't moved. The pack didn't know I was there, like a rabbit that a hound can pass a foot away, so long as the rabbit doesn't twitch. No, the dogs didn't see me. They wanted the stew. Cerberus and Rin Tin Tin inched forward. Snow White was behind them, her nose up scenting the air. The Seven Deadly Sins came up to the pot and ate greedily. I was surprised. I had always heard about alpha dogs and how they would eat first. But here the obviously strongest dogs gave way to the weakest. I wondered if the stories of alpha dogs were just a way of us projecting our own humanity—inhumanity I should correctly say—on these poor, maligned pooches.

The seven puppies ate. Snow White and her two guardians shared. The rabble came up and pushed each other in an orderly way, pawing the sand to get every taste. I rolled quietly on my stomach. Little Scruffy Terror, half as big as the others, tolerated, pushed in between long legs. Where was Huckleberry? Cerberus looked in my direction. Maybe he was looking at me. Listening for me? But as subsequent events proved, probably not. He angled his head and stiffened his pointed ears. He was the very image of Satan in a soft glow of embers. It occurred to me that Satan too has his minions, and for them he is hero. What judgment could I make on the sins of the fallen? On all the Harrys and Jacks and Neals and sad, old stumblebums who live out their lives on the Row? Snow White paused and raised her ears. Rin Tin Tin gave a low growl, and the others stopped their eating, the pups perplexed. I tensed thinking they had sensed me and would attack. Where was Harry? Had he stumbled up? Was he the object of Satan's wrath? I shifted to clear my line of sight. No, he was still curled immobile on the sand. His eyes were wide open. What was he seeing?

Quietly, the crack of embers. Then softly in the distance, pianissimo, the opening bars. Baying. Bawling of distant hounds. It was eerie to hear other dogs. Soft cries came from across the lake. I heard a engine far away, a standard transmission shifting, up, down, revving. Then moving closer and closer, crescendo. Headlights, like fireflies in the woods on the far side of the water, bouncing and moving fast on a road that I didn't know was there. Another engine followed and more headlights bouncing and the sound close enough to hear a tailgate banging. I could see headlights racing through the trees. The whole area must have been interlaced with dirt roads. "What the hell?" Thought but not spoken aloud, primordial instinct to quiet, to hide. I had no idea. Locals drunk and racing on the back roads? Another car, loud, racing up the road we had come in on? The dirt road where we had been dropped off? Locals come to party? Maybe they could help get us out of here. Give Harry some booze. Lights stopped across the water. Two sets of lights and I heard voices I could not decipher. They seemed to have stopped. But the baying dogs were getting close. I lay still on my stomach feeling vulnerable. What was going on? Someone coming up the dirt road, roaring up. I could see some flashes of headlight. Then the engine quieted. They'd found the trash pile. The engine up again, backing I supposed. Something ran between myself and the lake. The hounds were close, very close. The puppies understood and ran for the boathouse. I could only lie still and watch. My pack stood with tails straight and hair up. Quiet. Waiting.

A loping stride, moving with haste, yet seeming unhurried, a skinny dog-like body, an oversized, bushy trailing tail that I could see silhouetted against the white beach sand. Not a dog? It was running along the shore into the shallows. Fox! It took me a moment to process the information.

My dogs, my feral pack, understanding better than I did what was coming, discounting the fox, stood their ground. What could the well-fed sporting dogs have thought? They didn't expect a fight. No. All they knew was the terror-stricken fox fleeing and their sport of the chase. No blame to them, it was all they knew. But did they have any sense of what they were running into? The hunting hounds ran right into us. Across the clearing, the pack splitting around the firepit, my dogs on them, pushing them to confusion. I rolled to my knees and scrambled to the fire, threw dead, dry sticks on red coals. Resin-saturated twigs smoldered. I threw on more. White smoke, dense, rose and danced. Dogs barking and baying and yelping all around me. Pitiful cries of pain. Then, flash as the tinder caught and exploded all at once in a blaze of light. Hounds crazy-fixed on the fox with noses down trying to find the scent. Scruffy Terror on a hound with jaws locked and the hound, shaking-ferocity, eyes of fear in the firelight, trying to get the little beast off of him. Bawling. Barking. Circling the firepit. Screaming with panic. My dogs, territory compromised, defending their home, defending their own, defending their young. White spotted hounds crashing into dark forms of doberman and shepherd and rabble of frightened, vicious, nameless pariah mongrels who had found haven in the pines. A hound down on its back and Cerberus standing over it, fear incarnate. I turned away. Pitiful Huckleberry, not so long removed from the hunting pack, perhaps this one, standing and baying, torn between two worlds. The old mother stood in the door of the boathouse, now Kali, not Snow White, we had named her wrong, Goddess of Death watching the destruction with wild, lustful eyes, spittle-soaked lips, last line of protection for her pups. Harry immovable, dogs jumping over him, "Don't move," not heard in the commotion. And me standing by the blaze, almost burning, dogs ignoring me. Rin Tin running by, grabbing the hamstring of some poor pooch and the pooch going down, rolling, up running into the pines with flowing black blood, stumbling on three legs, wailing. The fire's blaze, cries in the night. Hounds fleeing into the trees, hunters hunted, their chase broken. Fox forgotten. Chaos reigns. A bodhisattva smiles. And a tired, frightened, bushy-tailed creature finds a fox's salvation, disappears into the night, believer at last in a fox's God.

I threw more wood on the fire.

Harry was up running, stumbling, falling. "Shit." The dogs with their chase instinct in gear would kill him. What should I do? Tackle him? Stop him somehow. The dogs were in the woods, pursuing the pursuers. He ran past Kali, still defending the boathouse door, teeth glistening in the blazing light.

She didn't give chase, thank God. Where were the others? Harry ran into the lake. "Can't ya hear 'em?

"Hear 'em?" he cried. "I'm coming to ya."

I could hear 'em. Not the full-formed baying like before, but broken, frantic cries in the night as the domestic pack tried to find itself and the feral pack gave chase.

Into the lake? Maybe he was thinking to break the scent like the fox? Maybe he was just running forward and the lake happened to be in that direction? He splashed into the water and fell knee deep. He sat up. "Jesus Jesus Jesus."

"Harry," I called softly. "It's okay. They're gone. It's the fox. They're after the fox."

"Do ya hear 'em? Hear 'em?"

"They're leaving."

"The children. Don't ya hear 'em? Crying. Crying a song." He stood and started to walk along the shore. Stumbling in the knee-deep water, shoeless, soaking wet. Pausing now to cock his head to determine the direction. Falling in the lake weeds, disappearing under the water, sitting shoulder deep in the shallows. Rising haltingly to fall again and crawl with his head just above the surface. Then up on his feet and turning back and heading to the boathouse on shore. Stopping and listening. Moving off again into the lake. Stopping as the water came up to his chest. "Can't say. Say where they is."

"Harry, you're going to drown!"

And had he fallen again he probably would have drowned. I didn't want to go into the water, but I saw no choice. I waded out to get him.

"Tell me. The children. Where are the children?"

There weren't any children.

"In the shadows. See 'em." I couldn't tell if Harry was talking to me—trying to show me the children—or he was talking to himself. Or to the children. "Come out. Come out. Ain't gonna hurt ya."

"Harry, there're no children. It's dogs. A pack of dogs running a fox." But he wasn't listening to me, only to his hallucinations.

"I don't see 'em no more. I hear 'em. They's having a party."

The children were as real to him as the baying dogs were to me.

"Jesus, I'm sinking. Quicksand boy. Quicksand got me."

It wasn't quicksand. It was muck and mud and leaves fallen into a hole, but I didn't know that and neither did Harry. It stumbled him and he fell. I considered for a moment that quicksand would have solved *my* problem. But we were a team and I reached out to help, sunk to my waist and after a second of panic on my own part, felt a solid bottom of sand. I yanked him up by the shoulder. Rougher perhaps than was appropriate. I was mad at the whole situation. This was not the idyll I had anticipated. I was also scared of the dogs and of what was to come and Harry's condition. I had Harry's arm in my hand and tried to drag him back toward the fire.

He shook me off and turned to listen. He tripped, stumbled into the hole again and from its depths came up with two handfuls of decaying weeds. The stench of death—or stench of life reborn, I don't know—both I guess—but the smell sticks with me now, and I can recall it as I write this, and I recall Harry's dark night.

He fell to his knees, squeezed the mud through his fingers and held the black, stinking weeds up to the sky.

I had an idea.

"Over there," I said. "By the fire. I see them."

"Where?"

I pointed toward the fire. "The children." He listened and pointed toward the far end of the lake. "No, by the cabin." I wanted to get him out of the lake.

"Let's go find 'em.

"I don't see 'em," he said when we reached the fire. His face was a madman's. Hair wet and dripping and him shivering. "You heard 'em. Said ya did."

I hadn't heard them. But Harry did. He kept turning to listen to pinpoint the source, but couldn't because the voices were in his head. "I see 'em in the shadows." He took two steps, staggering steps toward the dogs, which were in the brush, having given up the chase. I didn't know how the dogs would react while they were still stirred up from the sporting pack. I took Harry's arm, gently this time, and he stopped, sat, shook his head—a man can only stand so much—and said, "Ain't no children."

"No."

"I don't feel so good."

In the flaring pine logs—I had a good, bright, strong fire going—Harry shook. But the shaking this time was different, quicker, more contained, and with a kind of rigidity. His eyes flicked to the side, and his head cocked over and twitched. His mouth opened and jerked like he was trying to say something that had been forgotten long ago, spittle was on his chin. He fell over. The sand stuck to the side of his face and to his wet clothes. His eyes came back, and he looked at me. "I ain't going yet. Please, Jesus, don't let 'em put in no box. Not yet." He turned on his side without rising and retched and retched, retched until a pool of blood and vomit glistened in the light of the flame.

I don't know how long I waited. He lay on the sand panting like an exhausted hound. I was at a loss. "Do you want some water?" I asked. I didn't know what else to do.

I got him some water and helped him sit up, and he took the cup and held it with two hands, shaking.

"Gonna beat this thing. Ain't going in no box yet."

I had to admire him.

He was shaking again. I put wood on the fire. I offered him coffee. I offered water. I had no experience. I didn't know what to do. He shook. I thought it was the wet clothes. I told him to take them off and went into the cabin and got some fresh pants and a shirt and a blanket. He stripped in front of the fire, and when I saw him I turned my head. A skinny guy, so pale and bruised with scars on his back. He was a naked, broken man. What he had once been, time and alcohol had taken.

He dressed in the fresh clothes with some difficulty. His legs trembled and he had trouble putting them into the pant legs. I remember how he had to sit on the sand. No underwear. I hadn't brought any. Before the fire, with a blanket around his shoulders, he still shook and sweated simultaneously. He sat with the small of his back against a low log and starred into the fire. He was waiting for it to end.

Harry was enduring. We heard the hounds in the distance. Sometimes the sounds and the headlights came bouncing on the road across the lake. Maybe I should have gone and tried to flag them down. But I thought that we'd be ok. A pickup speeding through the night, tires on gravel invisible on a back road. Harry asking for confirmation at each sound. "Ya hear that?" "Yes." Who knew what was out there? Men missing teeth, loaded with hard cider and shotguns and a distinct dislike of college students? And what we had done to their dogs. Who knew what reception we would get?

The stars moved. I put logs on the fire and they were consumed. I understood that time was passing. But it seemed all stood still. And, Harry, I could only imagine then what he was feeling.

Sometimes he'd close his eyes, but not for long. "When I close 'em I see things," he said.

"Them children? Hear 'em?"

"No." I didn't hear them.

"Them dogs?"

"Yes, I hear them."

"Somebody having a party."

"No Harry, nobody's having a party."

In his own way he was coherent for a time. He said that he knew the children weren't really there. But maybe? Part of him knew that they were, perhaps, real. It was something you knew wasn't true, he tried to explain, but might have been. The kind of thing that goes against all the evidence. "Man wins a lottery," Harry said. "Seen it happen." Of course, the odds of it happening to *you* were pretty slim. "Man gets sober." Same thing, the odds were slim. "Maybe them children were here a long time ago. Happy before that sporting man turned to the bottle. Maybe we's hearing their echoes." It was all crazy, trying to put logic into what would not hold logic, like squeezing the dead, stinking lake bottom through his fingers, rationality slipping into to full-blown crazy. Maybe it made sense to him? What could I do? I kept the fire up. Kept the dogs away. Harry cried, sobbed an apology for something from his past. He swore at a brother he had lost long ago. "Momma died. Never said. Never told me. Come home one day. Looking for my momma. Gone. Strangers in the house. Man said 'Get out. Get away you bum.' Sold my house. Momma gone. Gone in the ground. People living there don't know no Harry.

"Man give me beer. Drank 'em after hard days. Good man's pleasure. Drank whiskey in my morning mug. What the hell! What the hell? I knew it then. Knew it then. God damn. Damn God.

"Jesus, I'm scared.

"Don't know what happened, son. Got me off course. Course gone off. Took a drink one morning in a mug. Coffee with whiskey. Felt good. Good idea. Ain't nothing wrong with that. Good man's vice. Off course, off to the races. Steer 'er full and by. Full and by my son.

"Liked them places. Bright and dark. Sparkling off them bottles. Sparkling pretty. Gonna be different tonight.

"Never gonna be different. Always the same. Guess I liked it that way. Same. Same. She took the kids. Never come home. Light and dark. Shine and shadows.

"I coulda fought it, son.

"Only been something to fight. Woulda fought it. KaPow. Right in the kisser. Never back down from a fight. Weren't no fight. No fight. Gimme something to grab and hold. Tear 'em, tear 'em apart. Gimme a wall to put my back against. Something solid under my feet. Gimme a place to set and stand. Gimme a star to steer her by. Gimme a man stand back-to-back. Oh Jesus. Damn Ya.

"Damn Jesus. Where was Ya?

"Used to be brave. Scared. Scared all the time. All feared up.

"Free man. Never tie me down. Ain't going in no ground. Get out damn box!

"Mother of God. What's happening to me!

"I jus' can't figure it out.

"Save yourself men. Save yourself. Abandon ship. She's ah going down.

"Steer her full and by. Full and by boys. Don't give up the ship. 'Do you strike your colors, sir?' No, damn Ya. Just begun to fight. Bombs Away." And he was off again and into the lake shouting at the night and the stars and the finite sky.

"You was once a man.

"Have You forgotten?

"Forgotten what it's like to be a man?

"Damn Ya. Show Yourself. Face me Ya damn Thing. Damn Jesus. Show Yourself Ya damn Sonofabitch!"

He was sobbing now.

"Show Your face."

"Damn You. Sonofabitch. I ain't going. You mean old Bastard."

"You was a man.

"Ain't *You* never had no thirst?"

He stopped knee deep. I guess the cold water shocked him back to whatever reality he was capable of. I was just getting dry, glad not to have to get him. He was done. He came back and sat down.

I wonder still, now, today, why the men in their pickup trucks running the pack didn't see the fire and investigate. Fire in the pines is no joke. All I can think is that they saw and thought it was just the local kids partying. I wonder what would have become of me, and of Harry, had they shown up to rescue us? Where would I be now if Harry hadn't shown me the way? And Harry, would he have gone on in his misery, forever unredeemed? It seems a miracle to me now, a miracle that Harry and I were permitted to take our little passion play to its finale.

# the gift of grace

"Damn it to Hell," quietly spoken when he opened his eyes.

Static on this page, words bear slight resemblance to the man who lay on the sand next to the dying fire. Words can tell you that he was a hopeless drunk. A rummy of the first degree. Drinker of spirits. Crusher of souls. Souse. Sot. Stumblebum. Boozer. Not a hardworking hobo. (Weed your garden for a meal mister?) No *King of the Road*. Not a tramp, tramping over the next rise to find, what?—I didn't know. He was a God damn lush. A lousy drunkard who'd pick the frozen pint from the pocket of a dead friend. Call him a dipsomaniac if you want to be formal about it. A toper. Or maybe a break-your-heart, back-alley wino like Kerouac before he went on the harder stuff and became a whiskey-drinking bhikku.

But after all the words he was still Harry. And Harry was in a bad way, a really bad way.

For myself, I just wanted to be done with it, done with him and his boozing. It had been a hard night. I was tired and frightened. That conscience (Proof of soul?) was weakening. Selfishness battled selflessness, inhumanity fought humanity. I was only human, and Harry was beyond human help. He was doing his best, curled on the sand with arms under his head to make a pillow, eyes wide staring into the gray before dawn, spasms of trembling passing through his body.

We'd both fallen asleep out by the fire, at least I had. I don't know if Harry dozed or simply closed his eyes. I had tried to get him to go into the cabin, but he wouldn't. Something about being inside scared him. Bunks like coffins. "Ain't going in no box." When I opened my eyes the world was dim. My clothes were wet with dew. I got up and rinsed my face and made my coffee while he lay on his side, big eyes watching. What was he seeing?

Damn drunk.

He and that Christian girl and that French-speaking co-ed and all that talk of Montréal. They'd gotten me into all this. And Kerouac, what the hell? I had believed them all. What had happened? Why was I here with this pathetic drunk? Where was my sweet port? The girls and the poets?

He was up staggering and cursing, almost standing, but his legs so bad that he fell over, crawling to the woods to relieve himself. I watched him trying to pee on his knees and holding to a tree, and me, turning my gaze to the lake and the cruel dawn—promise of the new day.

I expected him to return to the fire, but he crawled behind the boathouse, "to die alone like a dog," I thought. I heard him moving rubbish and muttering. He hadn't given up, was still looking for a lost bottle of booze. Incredible, insatiable, insane—he couldn't walk, but he was still looking. I built up the fire. My dew-wet shirt gave me a chill. I rubbed my chin. I had started itching. This whole beat and busted thing was losing its appeal. What the hell was Harry doing? I heard him in the boathouse. Had he crawled through the dogs' hole?

I was ready to go look for him when he appeared. "Gonna party with the Lady." He lurched from the frame of the boathouse door to the first sapling. Small cans cradled in an arm, the other reaching for the stability of the young tree, but falling into it. His legs just gone, spilling him to the sand. I might have helped. He crawled toward the firepit. "Harry, give it up," thought, but mercifully, not stated. He was an amazing thing to watch. He moved against his will, some spirit animating his actions. He crawled past me, struggling to hold his precious cargo and move forward toward the lake. He put the cans down on the sandy shore and paused, on his knees, turned to me. "Need something to put it in. Maybe you find me that jar?"

He was too pathetic. I had to help. I got the mayonnaise jar for him. His yesterday's tee-shirt, wet and crumpled, was just out of arm's reach. He leaned over for it, lost his balance and fell in the sand. Rolled on his side to get back up. The cans had lids like a paint can. Harry needed to pry them off. He didn't even try, simply held one up and back without turning his head as a way of indicating my assistance.

The Lady in question, the Pink Lady, was Sterno, a.k.a. canned heat—food-warmer of buffet caterers and fire-starter for rainy-day campers. It's jelled alcohol that burns with a hot, blue, translucent flame. And for some reason I don't understand, is colored pink, hence the name. Not an odd item to find in an old hunting camp. Alcoholic aficionados of the Lady filter it through a rag, supposedly to get out the poisons, but really to turn it from jell to drink. Mixed with anything to cut the taste, or taken straight, it's the cocktail of last resort for the desperate.

I got a screwdriver and helped him by opening the cans, then went back to my coffee. He was sobbing softly. There was no joy, not like the found bottle of beer from the pile of party trash or the Scotch I had produced from the rubbish. He'd been excited about them—this was different. I left him alone. He'd be drunk again. Maybe dead? Maybe blind? Wasn't that what happened? My knowledge of Sterno was incomplete.

Then what? How long would we be stuck here? I had half a mind to smack him. I was all for shouldering my pack and walking out and leaving him on his own to drink himself blind. He scooped the pink gel out with his fingers and put a handful in the shirt. He made a bag of the cloth and squeezed it carefully, catching the drippings in the wide mouthed jar. He was meticulous, scraping out each can, doing good for a guy with trembling hands. He had three cans. He went with his finger around the inside edges to to get it all. I suppose he was fighting panic, perhaps putting off the moment it would be done and drunk and gone. It took so long. I had to turn away. I felt ashamed to be watching him. I didn't want to see him drink it. I stared into the fire with my own selfish thoughts. If it killed him, would it be my fault? Should I stop him? Could I stop him? What would he do? I almost did—stand up and go to him and grab it out of his hand and throw it onto the lake. Did I know better? Where was my soul? What should I do? To this day I am convinced that an unseen hand held me back. This was something that Harry had to do himself.

Lost in the fire and my own thoughts, the splash turned my head. Concentric circles fading. He'd flung the mayonnaise jar into the lake. The cans followed. His shoulders were shaking. He was on his knees with his hands pressed together, eyes upturned. I hear him now, softly, almost imperceptibly, a whisper, zephyr in the stillness.

"I'm asking Ya."

Poor Harry.

He straightened up for a moment, then relaxed and slumped back down, still on his knees.  Sobbed quietly. It was all rather odd. I sipped my coffee, took a drag on my cigarette, felt the guilt of a reluctant voyeur. It was sad to see him broken.

Now, how do I write this?

It's easy to write despair. I think you can understand, and perhaps feel, the broken man that Harry had become.

But that morning?

How can I write that dawn? Or any dawn? For dawn is a promise, each dawn is yours, personal and private. And this particular dawn, Harry's dawn, cannot be fully captured with words—evoked only in those who know.

Now, I ask you to remember your dawn.

I remember mine.

Thirty years have passed. I am nearing fifty—drunken and broken as Harry was drunken and broken. Yet another dawn enters. A sun rises over the sea. I cannot go on. I look into the empty bottle. Without faith. Without hope.

I remember Harry.

And I ask.

In that moment everything changes. Grace arrives ever so softly, but arrive it does.  And I am certain of that which cannot be—but surely is. Something I do not understand answers my plea. The obsession that has held me for three decades is lifted. I know as I reach out my hand that it will be grasped in return. And I will have peace. The same peace that Harry was given that dawn.

Now, that said. Now, how do I tell you about that morning of Harry's? How do I write the dawn that greeted a new life? It's been almost forty years since that dawn with Harry, and a decade since I took *my* last drink, since *my* dawn, when I asked and was delivered. And now as I write this memory, I still don't fully understand. I suppose that all I can do now is describe what happened.

I left him alone while the sun bled through the trees. I made some fresh coffee and offered it to him. He didn't move or speak for an eternity. The sun stood above the trees, up bold and full and shone in our faces. A second sun reflected in the water, bright as the first. Both blinding in still air on still water. Harry looked at me with teared cheeks and pure eyes.

"I didn't drink it."

I looked at Harry. It was Harry—no doubt about it —same clothes and hair and facial features. Who else? But it was like I had never seen him before.

"Didn't drink it."

He struggled to stand. He'd been on his knees without moving for, how long?  An hour? Two? More?

"Gonna be alright."

I reached down. Took his hand.

"He told me."

I put my other hand under his arm to help him rise as gently as I could and felt his tremors resonate through my body.

"I'm cold." He was sweating. "I'm real cold."

"I'll get a blanket."

"Ya got some coffee?"

"Sure," I said. I didn't understand what was happening.

I helped him sit by the fire. I got a blanket to wrap his shoulders, handed him half a mug of coffee.

"Ain't got no cream?" he asked with a weak smile. He knew we didn't. "Maybe some sugar?"

"There's some sugar left. I'll get it," I said.

"That'd be nice," said with that same weak smile. "You been holding out."

Harry liked his sugar.

He had to jerk the mug up to his mouth with both hands and hold it against his lip to stabilize it enough for him to take a sip, just like the not-fermented failure of the night before. When the sweet coffee hit his stomach he puked it right back up. He shook noticeably. His hands and his legs would jerk in spasms, relax, then shake again—his mouth, still red from the iodine—had an odd, little twitch. He smelled awful. He lay with his back against a log and looked at the lake. I took the mattress from his bunk and made him as comfortable as I could. He didn't want to go inside.

"Pretty morning," he said. "Prettiest morning I ever saw. Don't hardly deserve it.

"Never noticed that tree. See how that one's all crooked. And that other one is kinda straight and all. Each one. All different. All them greens. Who knew there were so many greens. Look, that one's got big balls of needles, like a Christmas tree. Guess that's where they got the idea."

I boiled water, then cooled it in the lake. I didn't know what to do but to give him water. I didn't want him drinking the lake water straight. Maybe boiling would kill the germs. Coffee he just puked right back up. I did whatever I could to help him. But it wasn't much. I had no experience with drunks and delirium tremens or strokes. He'd had a stroke, that's what I decided. He'd gone mad. It seemed to me to be a sad business. I had tea bags and made him weak tea. I thought that he should eat, but the idea of the ration food turned even my stomach. He'd have to wait until we could make a run for it. I guess, in retrospect, I should have gone out on the highway, walked until I could flag down a car, get Harry some help. But Harry kept saying that he'd be okay. And something about his attitude, even as he shook and sweated and stunk, made me believe him. Mostly, he didn't want me to leave him alone.

A voice had come softly and whispered over his shoulder, "You gonna be okay."

"Jesus," he said, had spoken to him. "Maybe ain't Jesus," he corrected himself, he wasn't too sure. "Might be God, an angel, even the Virgin. Momma said She'd help me." Or maybe something that he didn't know, "Buddha or Somethin'?" But It *had* whispered over his shoulder as he kneeled and prayed. That's all. But that was enough. "Taking care of me. Takin' care of ol' Harry."

The lake went on like nothing had happened. Birds flew across the open sky. Fish made circles that spread and faded as if they had never been. A dark, crested bird with a loping flight dropped down and brought up a silver minnow. And Harry smiled through the whole thing. The lake hadn't changed, but Harry had.

"Them little bugs. What ya call 'em? Gnats. See 'em? Looks like two, but really one and a reflection. One ain't really there."

There was a myriad of gnats flying inches above the glass-smooth water. A gray butterfly, small as a dime, fluttered into the light just right and turned a distinctly delicate blue.

"Like the children," I said, referring to the voice that had whispered to him. "The voice?"

"No." he said. And he was quite sure.

"Different.

"Something I know sure as everything. More than anything."

He was stupid happy. His mind was cracked. I'd never seen a man go insane right before my eyes. If he hadn't been so emaciated, if he could have taken more than three steps without falling over, I might have been frightened of him. It was clear that he needed a drink. I had seen the day before how a drink or two would bring him back to normal. I wished I had one. He shouldn't have thrown away that Pink Lady—crazy coot.

"Fifty years I've been wanting ah drink. Waking up. Going to sleep. Even when I'm drinking, I'm wanting ah drink.

"Drunk I'm wanting ah drink. No more. Why do ya think that is?"

"A broken blood vessel in his brain, a clot cutting off some chunk of his mind," I thought, but did not speak.

"Used to be thinking always, always thinking where I'm getting the next drinking, where the last drinking went. Thinking about people done me dirty. People I done dirty. Round and around, old head spinning. Ain't spinning no more. Can't tell ya how. I always wanted to know why. Know it now."

"Why? What? Know what?" I wanted to know too, he said it with such assurance that for a minute I was sucked into his madness.

"Ya jus' know it. Pretty here, ain't it?"

"How do you know it? What is it?"

"Been looking in a bottle. Bottle don't know nothing. Didn't know where to look. 'Found it in an empty bottle,' man said that. Didn't know what he was saying. Know it now. Know what he was saying. Gonna have to look him up. Froze to death he did."

"You saw God?"

"Didn't see nothing. Jus' kinda know. Like them dogs in the woods. Can't sometimes see 'em, but we knows. Smell 'em. Smell my momma's cooking too. Know she got supper cooking. Momma always cooking something. Got a dollar for poor Harry."

I didn't understand, but I could see that it was different. The voices of the children frightened him, filled him with panic. Now he was calm. This new voice affected him differently.

"Pretty as a picture," he said. "Trees and water and fishes and birds and even the little bugs that ya can't hardly see, all happy like the fingers on ma hand." He held his hand out and opened and closed his fingers to demonstrate, and the shaking took over and his hand twisted and didn't respond and shook until he had to draw it back and push it down between the mattress and his body.

"No hope for old Harry. Worthless old bum, ain't worth the Lord's salvation," he said grinning like it didn't matter. "No hope and not to matter. Too late for me, son. Son, you got to jump this ship. Abandon ship. Jump. No need for you go down with her. I'll be along presently," all said serenely, slowly with a smile—that stupid, placid, Christian girl smile. "You ask Him," she had said.

It was a brain hemorrhage. That was the only explanation I could understand. I looked carefully at his face for signs of drooping. What I saw instead, and it sounds insane to say, with his wild hair and blotchy skin, red-stained mouth, emaciated stinking body, distended stomach—he was as beautiful as any person I had ever seen. I can still see him and still doubt what I see. His eyes were different. They were clear and relaxed. I saw the soft blue iris instead of the blood-streaked white. And something about his mouth—still stained comically, tragically, with the iodine—his pure smile, the smile of a baby. I remember the bags, so prominent under his eyes, were gone. Like I said, it was all so weird. I began to doubt myself and for years afterward continued to disbelieve. "Maybe," I thought, "I'm the one with the brain hemorrhage."

"I heard Him. 'Gonna be okay.' It ain't like them hallelujah boys say, not like that. It's all quiet. Him just 'taking my hand.' Taking Harry's poor shaking hand in His."

Harry was dying. He needed booze. I offered to look in the rubbish pile. He waved me off. I was disappointed and irritated and more uncomfortable with Harry than when he was drunk. The whole God idea bothered me, touched something essential and raw.

He lay on his side watching the lake. For a time he hummed a little tune. I asked what he was thinking. "Nothing," he said. "Nothing to think."

I don't know how long I sat with him, long enough that I had to pee again. The dogs were lurking in the bushes, so I went the other way around the cabin. I was, or maybe wasn't, surprised to kick an empty bottle, then another and another. I'd found the El Dorado of empties we had been seeking. I pushed around with my foot and found what I knew would be there—a bottle of salvation with its cork in it, half full. I peed. Then picked the bottle up and uncorked it and smelled it. It smelled ok, and I took a modest pull for myself. That crazy, old coot was right. He'd been on-target with his role playing about the man who tossed the bottles. Harry's only mistake was that the man must have been left handed, and Harry threw with his right. Harry was right about God too. God had saved him with this bottle of booze. It was just what we needed to get Harry up and out of this hellish hunting camp.

I hide the bottle behind my back and surprised him with it like a birthday gift. He looked at it long and hard, maybe even drooled a bit. He leaned forward and up and rolled himself onto his knees and reached out his hand, looked closely.

"That what I think it is?"

I took the cork out. Took a little sip. It was Scotch. No doubt about it. I had learned a bit over the last couple days. With the cork out, I offered it to Harry.

He snatched his hand back. "No, son."

He rolled over and turned his back toward me and his face away from the booze. "No. You keep it for yourself. I'm done."

I couldn't believe it. He needed it. I could understand throwing away the canned heat, but this was good Scotch. I corked it and put it down. Poor Harry.

I sat with him until he closed his eyes. Maybe he was asleep.

I wanted to think. I wanted to figure it all out. Harry was in no shape to move. How long would it take for him to get so he could walk? Who would stop for someone looking as bad as he did? I'd have to clean him up. Maybe I could tell the driver that he was my grandfather or something, that we were camping and he'd gotten sick or something? I was trying hard to think of a way out. There's always a way to think it out, at least that's what I believed then. I needed a story. I needed a narrative to understand and explain what was happening. Was Harry's smile evidence of a God I didn't see? Was it the ripple that spread and faded into nothing, yet gave faith to the fisherman? I shook my head—shook off my thinking. "I've been in the pines too long when I start to believe that some stupid drunk is talking to God—and God is talking back to him," said aloud to the lake and trees and fish unseen. I needed to get back to civilization. I wanted a drink, to open the bottle and drink it down. But we might still need it. If I could get him to drink it, maybe we could still walk out.

He opened his eyes with a start. There was panic in them. "Children. Hear 'em. They's out there. We gotta find 'em. We gotta tell 'em. Devil's out here. Jersey Devil!

"Oh God, what's happening to me? Jesus, don't leave me."

He was up and stumbling toward the lake.

"Them children. You hear 'em?"

"Harry, there's no children."

He paused for a moment.

"Maybe? I'm thinking that there may just be?"

"If there were, I'd hear them too."

"They're laughing. Laughing and singing. Happy children. Maybe having a party?"

"No Harry. No children."

"Maybe just?"

"Maybe just no."

"You hear 'em too?" Harry said excitedly, misunderstanding my words.

"May just be?" he said quietly. "I kinda know it ain't real, but maybe it is? I hear's 'em laughing and calling, but can't quite make out what they say. Maybe they're calling to me?"

"No Harry, it was the dogs. No children. No Jersey Devil," I almost continued with, "No God either," but something stopped me. Maybe I didn't want to be mean again. Maybe I didn't want to take away his hope. Maybe something else? What I said was, "As soon as you're a little stronger we'll get out of here."

Harry shook his head no and laughed quietly.

"No children. No Jersey Devil. I know that. I know that. I know what.

"DTs. Got them DTs. Got 'em bad."

It was heartbreaking, but I was secretly relieved. Miserable, incoherent Harry made sense—that was a story I could believe.

"What day it is?

"Lake don't matter what day it is. Dog don't matter what day it is.

"Been studying on it," he continued.

"Maybe it's not God. Maybe it's that ol' Devil." And he looked into the trees as if the Jersey Devil was in there waiting for him.

"Devil offering me a bottle. I seen him. You was gone. Devil was here. Holding out his hand."

I showed him the bottle I had found. "It wasn't a dream. I found you a bottle."

He rolled over, turned away from me. "Don't want it. Don't need it. You just leave ol' Harry to his peace. Satan, get behind thee."

I put the bottle behind, out of sight. "I'm sorry Harry.

"Harry, we've got to get out of here."

"Ain't no rush"

"I've got to get back to school."

"That's good, going to school. Don't be no drunk like me.

"It's a beautiful world, son. Almost missed it." His serenity had returned. His moment of doubt had passed. He looked like some ragged saint in the wilderness, placid, serene, at peace with the world and one with his God.

"We'll be getting out. You just get better. Get some sleep."

"Won't let me sleep.

"Been studying on things. Things when I shut my eyes."

Harry laughed.

He closed his eyes and described a bridge over a stream. It was made of wood, a simple log and stick bridge. Three children were leaning on the railing, the girl and the bigger boy were looking at a waterfall, a smaller boy was looking at the camera. The boys wore jeans. The girl wore red pants and a red shirt and, "A nice lady, she got a hat and gloves, and she's wearing pearls. My momma used to wear gloves. Wore a hat too. And she had pearls, always wore 'em to church. I remember that. She's getting out her pearls and putting 'em on for church. Used to hook 'em for her. She smelled so good. Ladies don't do that no more. Gentleman wore a hat. Always used to wear a hat. My daddy never left the house without a hat. Had a whole shelf of hats, nice hats. Not caps. Not caps like they wear today. Daddy never come home not wearing a hat.

"Get that fishing can! They's a nest of worms here."

There was nothing. "Them ol' DTs," he laughed. His brain was breaking up, and he was laughing about it. What else could you do? I looked at him. He needed booze. I offered him the bottle again and felt like the fallen one offering an apple to the innocence of Eve. But Harry was no innocent, he waved me off.

"Got a brother somewhere. Gonna look him up."

He sat and looked at the lake humming softly to himself. "It's a beautiful world," he said periodically. This said softly with quiet joy.

"Sister's dead, I think. Got to ask him. Ask my brother about my sister.

"Don't know where it went.

"Don't know where my life went.

"Thinking I'd have to be dead to feel this happy. Hard to remember being happy. Been so long.

"Scared all my life. Ain't scared now. Something strange, ain't it?"

There were extended pauses between his comments where he simply smiled and looked at the lake. I don't know that I can write this or how to explain his day. If you think it's all stupid—well maybe it is—but I was there. I saw it happen. There was contentment in him that I had never seen before. The bravado that had carried him all those years was gone. The tone of his voice, the meekness acquired, the smile beatific—it was the day he had been waiting for his whole life.

There is a verse in the Dharmapada that says that it is better to live one day in the Dharma than one hundred years in the darkness. All those years Harry had endured his darkness. Then when he had turned his beautiful eyes to the heavens on this, his morning, looking down in pity the Lord heard his cry and turned His gaze to meet Harry's. With this exercise of free will, this crying-out to something he did not understand, Harry had been graced with the quiet ecstasy of the mystic. He had discovered the living metaphysic of the philosopher, the singularity sought by the whirling Sufi, embraced the humility of the holy fool who wanders the white nights, experienced the satori of the Zen monk, seen the vision of the young brave who seeks *It* in the solitude of the Dakota badlands, taken the hand of the Christ, heard at last, the horn man's solo.

All it took was a lifetime of hard drinking and the profound act of asking.

"Don't know how it happened," Harry said softly. "Passes from drink-to-drink, day-to-day, week-to-week, year-to-year. Knew a day when I had a job, long time past, I was drinking then.

"I had a bottle full—whiskey it was—I drunk it down and didn't feel nothing. Something matter with this whiskey I thought, but it was me, something matter with me.

"Had a wife. 'Get out,' she says. Got out an' got a drink I did.

"Got a family. Maybe find 'em?

"See that? Big ol' fish hawk?"

"Yes." I did see it.

"Good. Me too. Thinking maybe I was 'maging it."

"No, I saw it too."

"Pretty out here.

"Ain't got no regrets. "Pretty out here. Pretty on the water."

"Yes."

Banal dialogue with the delivered.

One who had felt God's embrace—a man who's heard the voice of God—should have something better to say. Or so I thought.

Forgive my cynicism. I was young and didn't understand and didn't believe. "Harry, I'm sorry, you expressed yourself just fine."

The day passed.

I thought he was getting better, thought he'd pull through, but in the late afternoon Harry had another seizure. He came around, but his face remained twisted. He smiled and squeezed my hand. "You're going to be ok, Harry," I tried to reassure him.

"It's okay, son.

"Ain't got no regrets.

"Been a wonderful day. Wonderful day.

"Kinda makes it all worthwhile. Don't it?

"Daddy tossed his head back an' laughed.

"Momma always had a dollar in her apron for Harry.

"Ain't got no toes!

"Man ain't got no toes!

"Where'd they go?"

He had a final spasm. Opened his beautiful eyes.

"Ain't leaving ya, son. Just ask."

His eyes closed for the final time. He gripped my hand weakly. His breath slowed and slowed and slowed till it was a whisper, and I don't even know exactly when he left.

After such a hard life, to go so soft.

46959362R00113

Made in the USA
Middletown, DE
13 August 2017